REASON TO MURDER

REASON TO MURDER

R.A. Bennett

CHIVERS
THORNDIKE

This Large Print book is published by BBC Audiobooks Ltd, Bath, England and by Thorndike Press®, Waterville, Maine, USA.

Published in 2006 in the U.K. by arrangement with Robert Hale Ltd.

Published in 2006 in the U.S. by arrangement with Robert Hale Ltd.

U.K. Hardcover ISBN 1–4056–3709–9 (Chivers Large Print)
ISBN 13: 978 1 405 63709 1
U.K. Softcover   ISBN 1–4056–3710–2 (Camden Large Print)
ISBN 13: 978 1 405 63710 7
U.S. Softcover   ISBN 0–7862–8734–9 (British Favorites)

The text of this Large Print edition is unabridged.
Other aspects of the book may vary from the original edition.

Set in 16 pt. New Times Roman.

Printed in Great Britain on acid-free paper.

British Library Cataloguing in Publication Data available

Library of Congress Cataloging-in-Publication Data

Bennett, R. A. (Richard Alan), 1946–.
    Reason to murder / by R.A. Bennett.
      p.   cm.
    "Thorndike Press large print British favorites."
    ISBN 0–7862–8734–9 (pbk. : alk. paper)
    1. Ex-police officers—Fiction. 2. Private investigators—Fiction.
    3. Large type books. I. Title.
    PR6052.E5313R43 2006
    823'.92—dc22   2006010069

724893

CHAPTER ONE

The girl pulled her jacket tight to protect herself from the bitter wind. Her hair scattered and swirled about her face. She pulled it free where it caught in the corner of her mouth.

She seemed to have stood here in the darkness for hours, yet she knew it could only be a matter of minutes.

She heard a movement behind her and turned.

The cold tentacles of fear tightened around her heart. She opened her mouth and began to scream.

CHAPTER TWO

Monday, another short winter's day, the rain lashed against the window.

The alarm crashed at eight, and I tediously pondered on how to plug the next twelve hours. The answer came with a quiet, almost apologetic knock on the door below. It grew in volume, demanded attention.

Now, some time had passed, and I leaned forward. A sudden chill had pervaded the room despite the sickly warmth thrown from the gas heater. It sent ripples of unease along my spine.

And, as I listened, part of my mind was beginning to believe. In a hushed voice, the woman repeated her words.

'Karen died at fourteen minutes past four on the morning of the fourth of December. She saw the face of her killer. She called my name with her dying breath. That is the moment I awoke. I turned on the light and glanced at the clock. It was exactly four-fourteen.'

I stirred uncomfortably, aware that despite the icy coolness of my skin I had begun to sweat. I took the time to examine the couple seated opposite.

Both aged around sixty. She sat quietly, hands together as they twisted in her lap, eyes red but dried out, her crying done. It was the man who had tears in his eyes, lips whitened in grief. He glanced at her and they clasped hands. I lowered my eyes, embarrassed by such personal trauma. I had no words of comfort, no formula to ease the pain.

A nightmare? Is that what I should tell them? After all, there is no evidence of Karen dying, and certainly no body. Should I say Karen will turn up? Four days is not very long. I could conjure a hundred such platitudes, and none seemed appropriate.

And was I expected to take her words seriously? Had she experienced the violent death of her daughter?

2

I found the words to break the leaden atmosphere, going over old ground. 'And you say you have tried the police, Mrs Richardson?'

'Yes.' She took a deep breath. 'We came up yesterday. We talked with Val Spencer, Karen's friend, then visited the police station. A Sergeant Bell. A young man. He was patient and kind. He made a few enquiries, checked the hospitals. Nothing. There was little he could do. He didn't say so—but I got the impression he thought us rather silly. He took Karen's name, her description, and offered his regrets. It was he who recommended you if we wanted to pursue this matter further.'

Now why would Kevin Bell recommend this couple to me? The answer to that question intrigued me. I was finding it hard to meet the woman's eyes. I mumbled something about Kevin and I joining the police force on the same day, that he had been a little more successful. I needed more words, and fast. I was being sucked into the mire. The man, who had barely uttered a word since he entered the room, coughed into the back of his hand and reached inside his coat. He passed me a slip of paper.

A cheque for five hundred pounds made out to me. I stared at it a long time, bewildered. I had the sinking feeling I was being forced into something against my will. A twinge of irritation ran through me. I guess it showed in my face.

'Isn't it enough?' A puzzled frown creased the woman's forehead. 'We have more. We are not poor. Everything we have was for Karen. And now—'

I was close to tears myself, touched by the simplicity of their love and faith. I explained that it was too much. I offered to make a few enquiries, if only to prove them wrong—prove that Karen was still very much alive.

'Karen is dead,' the woman stated firmly. 'And of course you will keep the money, and whatever expenses you incur. Karen was murdered, Mr Conroy.' She raised a palm as I tried to interrupt. 'I demand that her murderer be brought to justice. That is why she called to me with her final breath. A plea for justice. I require you to find that person, and discover what was done with Karen's body. Then we can take her home and lay her to rest.'

Sweet Jesus! She almost had me believing, not whole heartedly, for a cynical voice at the back of my mind whispered that it couldn't be so, but I was surely believing it possible that she had experienced the death of her daughter from a hundred miles away. I fingered the cheque absently then slipped it into a drawer.

'I'll leave the cheque there for the time being, Mrs Richardson.' I forced myself to meet her eyes. 'If she's still in these parts—I'll find her.'

No further declaration of her daughter's

4

death. I asked if she had questioned Karen's old friends.

'We tried.' Now her eyes did begin to glisten. 'But as I told you, Karen had few friends. Always withdrawn and reserved. None of the girls she went to school with have seen her since she left Birmingham.'

'And that was eighteen months ago?' I asked. She nodded. 'And she came straight to this town?'

'Yes. I have tried to explain why she left.' Her eyes flicked to her husband. Then he stood and moved from the room. She remained, her voice dropping low. 'Don't judge us. We did what was best for Karen.' She rose to her feet. 'We are going home now. You have our phone number, and our complete confidence.'

She was gone, and the room began to warm. I heard the outer door close and their shuffling feet on the stairs, then the door to the street.

I leaned back, relaxed, allowed my eyes to wander over the office.

My world this. An old desk, one comfortable chair, two hard ones, a filing cabinet that contained few files, a divan couch on which I often slept, a gas fire. Almost thirty years old and I had thus reached so far. But it was enough for me.

And now I was about to embark on a search for a girl I had never heard of until an hour before; a girl whose mother believed her to be dead. And who was I to argue with that? Who was I to ponder on the inner workings of a mother's heart?

I studied the photograph of Karen that lay on the desk. Quite pretty, open faced, blue eyed, blonde hair touching the collar of a dark sweater. She was seventeen when this was taken, and if it hadn't been for the full breasts I'd have placed her age at no more than fifteen. Karen was now nineteen years old.

I glanced at my watch and pushed tiredly to my feet. No time like the present. I had nothing better to do.

CHAPTER THREE

Built towards the end of the last century, the mock Georgian terrace was not one of the town's worst eyesores, close, but not quite.

I climbed the five stone steps, relieved to be out of the driving rain. The gold plaque by the door spelled 'Ian Spencer—Interior Designs'.

I was inside, conscious of the puddles I was spreading on the thick piled carpet, feeling conspicuous and out of place.

Val Spencer, lifelong friend of the Richardson family and Karen in particular, was out, so I talked to her husband Ian. I liked him immediately; middle twenties, self-effacing, with a ready and boyish grin. We sat in his office and drank coffee.

'You will have to return when Val is here to get the more intimate details,' he was saying. 'She was the one closest to Karen.'

'But what was Karen like?' I insisted.

'Child-like in some respects, though intelligent.' He seemed perplexed by his own description. 'Yes, I'd say that was about right. Very quiet, very shy. We rarely spoke, and she never spoke about herself.'

'Did you like her?' I asked.

'Yes. I suppose I liked her. There was certainly nothing to dislike in Karen.'

'How did she come to be living here?'

'I thought the Richardsons explained,' he said warily.

'They didn't go into details.'

He nodded thoughtfully. 'Okay. My wife's family were friends of the Richardsons. Val knew Karen from the day she was born. There was trouble at home, and I'd rather you went into the details of that with Val. Mrs Richardson rang and asked if it was possible for Karen to come and stay with us for a while.

'Val and I had just married. We'd moved in here and were beginning to sort out the business. It was a little inconvenient, but we said okay. Karen stayed. With us at first. Then a flat on the top floor became available and she took it.'

'You didn't become personal friends?' I asked.

'No. Val seemed to be the only person she felt at ease with.'

I asked if Karen was attractive. He didn't need much time for thought.

'Yes. I'd say so, though she seemed very young. The body of a mature woman with the face of a young girl.'

It sounded a devastating combination to me. 'Did you notice a change in Karen over the last few days or weeks? Was she worried about anything? Her mother said she hadn't looked too well the last time she saw her.'

'Yes,' he said, after pondering a while. 'Over the past month or so. A little more withdrawn than usual, which is saying something. She lost weight. Sometimes she'd be quite perky. But most of the time tired and nervy, as if something was troubling her.'

'And what was troubling her?' I watched his head shake. 'You didn't question her?'

'No. I have tried to explain. It was impossible to get close to Karen. You learned not to question her.'

More questions from me. His answers were terse and to the point. She didn't bring boys home. He didn't know where she worked. I asked if Karen had mentioned why she was leaving.

'No,' he responded. 'I didn't know anything about it. Val told me next day, after she'd received that frantic phone call from Mrs Richardson. She mentioned Karen had said

8

something about leaving the day before. Val supposed that was exactly what happened— that Karen had packed her bag and left.'

There didn't seem to be much more to be had from Ian Spencer. We stood. He offered to show me the flat he shared with Val, assuring me it made quite a contrast to the grim exterior of the building, something that impressed potential clients. I declined, pleading a previous appointment. I commented that I wouldn't have thought there was much scope for his line of work in this town. He smiled.

'Don't knock this old place. There is still money floating around. I'm doing fine, though it is mainly offices and pubs. Once in a while I'm let loose on a real house, with real money to indulge my whims.'

We had reached the door, and parted with a handshake. I pulled my collar up and stepped into the rain. I'd be back later to meet his wife.

*   *   *

Wonderful!

The Forger was a pub created in God's image; all dark corridors, small dark rooms, comfortable chairs, twisted dartboards, soot on the darkened walls and ceiling from the coal fires.

Not many people around as I took my seat. A door opened and an elderly woman under a red beret peeped around. Her eyes swept over the room and lingered on me a moment, then she was gone. I soon forgot her.

I settled back. A thick wedge of steak and kidney pie before me, a cool pint to wash it down. I let the sounds of the pub wash around me, oblivious. I pushed the plate away, rested my eyes. I reached under the table to massage my knee. It had begun to ache earlier; a dull ache that often developed into a lancing pain.

Physiological, the doctors expounded.

Physiological? Balls! The ache was real, and when the pain was at its peak it turned my bowels to water. I took a steadying breath, and let my mind drift back.

Twenty years old again, bucking with life, proud, and arrogant as a rooster. April was receding into May, and in a couple of weeks it would be the great Wembley final, my first. I was already a county player, hotly tipped to make the Great Britain touring side. But that was far from my mind. Two weeks to kill before the great event.

A meaningless game, postponed from earlier in the season when the frost had bitten hard into the fixture list. Five minutes before I collected my first touch of the ball. A long pass I scooped up only inches from the ground. I was soon in full stride. I heard the crowd draw breath. This was what they paid their cash to see. Me! Frank Conroy!

I jinked inside the opposing centre. No

problem. Over the half-way line. Swerve left, outside the flat footed fullback. It was easy when you had wings on your heels. But the unexpected happened. A bare touch on the ankle and I was tumbling. Still, no great problem. I rolled onto my back, ready to spring up. I don't know where the bugger appeared from. I only knew he was suddenly there. My right knee took the full impact of his seventeen stone. I don't remember much after that, only the pain. But my Rugby League career was over.

Months later the doctors announced me fit. But I knew I wasn't. Hell! I limped like I had a wooden leg!

I was lost for a while after that.

I'd worked the sites since I was sixteen to build up my strength. No trade, no qualifications, only rugby. I filled in an application to join the police force. The medics appeared satisfied with my knee, and who was I to argue with the experts? I was a boy in blue.

I came out of my reverie and sank another pint, then plodded on my way, careful not to drag my leg.

*   *   *

I knew this town like the cracks on the ceiling in my office. I knew the buildings, the streets, the people, the pubs and clubs. But once

11

through the doors of this building I was on virginal territory.

Racks of books of every size and colour, the hum of whispered voices in the background, the scuff of shoes over the floor. There was a peculiar smell in the air, a strange mixture of paraffin and dust that made me want to sneeze.

I browsed, ran fingers along racks. Soon out of patience at my inadequacy, I called for assistance.

It came. Fresh out of school, pink cheeked and wide eyed, eager to please, she listened to my request with no hint of surprise.

I was soon seated at a table with a stack of books in front of me, my back turned to the old man whose hacking cough seemed intent on reducing the paper he held in shaky fingers to a pulpy mess.

I got down to business. I flicked through the books, then studied them more closely. I didn't know what I expected to find, possibly something to prove Mrs Richardson could not have experienced her daughter's death in the depths of sleep. But the evidence between the pages seemed to confirm the opposite, and almost invariably concerned women.

A woman arrives at the airport; a sudden fear grips her and she refuses to board the plane; the plane crashes.

A woman begs her husband not to drive to work; he laughs; he dies in a multiple car crash an hour later.

A woman decides to keep her child home from school; she doesn't know why; she later hears that the school bus has crashed; two children have lost their lives.

The list ground on endlessly. I found one case very similar to Mrs Richardson's.

A mother lies down for an afternoon nap; an hour later she is abruptly torn from sleep; she runs half a mile to the river bank; a crowd is gathered and she pushes through; there is a child lying on the wet earth; the child is her dead daughter.

I'd read enough. I pushed the books aside. And despite the impressive listing of evidence, I left that library still a committed sceptic.

*   *   *

I'd worked from this building. Old, worn, red Victorian brick and cold slate; icy in Winter, furnace hot in Summer, draughty all the year round; lots of corridors and worn tiles from a hundred years of heavy boots, humming electric fan heaters, sickly green walls; drab and forbidding, yet strangely welcoming to those who knew it intimately.

Two and a half years. Good and fulfilling years. I loved the force, the us against them syndrome. I was still part of a team.

I hadn't been a particularly good copper. If I'd stayed in I'd probably never have

13

progressed beyond the heady rank of constable. A simple, good natured plod, that would have been me. But the prospect didn't daunt me. I viewed the coming twenty years in relative contentment.

I was a sucker for the old sob story, that was my problem. String me a line and I was sure to buy it. A few carefully executed tears and I was reaching for my handkerchief. I sympathised with most people, from the harassed motorist to the discontented housewife who suddenly decides to brain her husband at the first whiff of perfume on his lapel. Still, I got along okay.

The knee did for me. The pain got worse. Sleepless nights and next day I'd be fit for nothing. And who the hell respects a Bobby with a limp? More doctors, more clicking tongues, more negative reports. Still they could find nothing wrong.

'Perhaps an appointment with a psychiatrist?'

Well, shove that up you know where!

The knee hurt! There was something inside that ground against bone. But nobody listened. Just another name on a chart. And now they were placing me in the land of the cuckoos. I resigned, and added my name to the ranks of the unemployed. Not yet twenty-four and stuck like a poxy guy on a dung heap. Even then I was out of luck. The Employment found me a job. And hell, what a job! But that was six years back.

I found the office, entered, sat, lit a cigarette, and waited patiently for the man behind the dcsk to acknowledge my presence.

He was Kevin Bell, detective sergeant; one of those rare individuals who smoked, ate, fornicated, and probably did everything else to excess and never seemed the worse for it. He passed exams with ease, and would probably make chief inspector in five years. He was just six months older than myself, and I envied him like hell.

He looked up and winked impishly. He pushed aside the papers he had been studying. In an easy and practised movement he caught the cigarette I tossed him.

'I take it they came—the Richardsons?' he asked, voice deep and casual as always, face momentarily disappearing in a cloud of smoke.

I nodded, and we talked, and we argued. We argued over everything, Kevin and I, but remained firm friends. We'd fought together with our backs to the wall against a gang of yobs and that meant everything.

'What are you carping about now, Frankie?' he rapped impatiently. 'Don't you think I'd have liked to have helped them?' He paused for confirmation but got none. 'She told the woman in the ground floor flat she was leaving. She packed a bag. And the girl is nineteen. Old enough. So Mrs Richardson wakes up in the middle of the night with a pain in her head. Her daughter's pain, she claims.

15

She believes she has experienced her daughter's death. Not only that, but that the daughter was murdered. Am I expected to mobilise a murder enquiry?'

I said calmly, 'I almost believe her.'

Kevin examined me, making sure it wasn't a leg pull.

'All right,' he said quietly. 'I have to admit she had the worms crawling up my spine for a while. But as soon as she left I shrugged it off. The same as you will when you decide to jump off the sanctimonious horse you're riding. The girl is off on a jaunt with a bloke. Find him, and you find her.' He drew breath, shrugged. 'And you know how it's been since the wages snatch at the Motor Works, and we've got nowhere with that. Ten days—and nothing.'

And didn't I just know. That particular robbery had been the biggest happening in this town since the Rugby League Cup Final I had so ruefully missed. But I wasn't interested in that. Kevin began to drum his fingers on the desk.

'Why are you here, mate?' he asked.

'To find out why you sent the Richardsons to me.'

'That should be obvious.' His eyes never flicked from my face. 'They need reassuring that their daughter is safe, and I knew you needed the business. Look into it for them. It shouldn't take you long to find the girl, once you discover who the boyfriend is.'

16

Close to the truth, but not quite there. He knew the Richardsons wouldn't let this drop, so he had shunted them on to me, as somebody in uniform had probably shunted them on to him. It was the way it worked. And it was obvious the Richardsons hadn't gone too deeply into Karen's background with him, or his attitude might have been a little different.

I left him to get back to his work.

CHAPTER FOUR

I waved to the lady behind the counter in the grocer's shop and turned into the narrow street at the side of the building. Through the door, up the narrow flight of wooden stairs. The walls were covered with posters of pop and film stars I'd bought for a pittance to cover the cracks in the plaster. It wasn't original, it didn't add class, but it surely brightened the place up. I heard the click of needles before I opened the door.

Mrs Harker sat in her easy chair. She looked up and smiled, then returned to her knitting.

She was in her sixties, pink cheeked, often testy, and in most ways the love of my life. A smashed hip as a result of a car accident had left her with a waddle that made a ruptured duck appear graceful. Two cripples together were me and Mrs Harker.

And she had inherited me. My mother's dying words had been, 'Take care of Frankie for me, Mary.' It was a bequest she took seriously. Aged sixteen, I moved into her home. Two years later I had a wife and was gone. Time rolled on. Six years of marriage, a divorce, and I was back at Mrs Harker's for another five years stint. I still had a room at her house, and often slept there.

And if I ever hankered after a secretary with silky golden tresses and tits like melons, I reconciled such dreams with the reality that sexy secretaries probably liked to receive pay cheques, and probably weren't much cop when it came to humping soiled bed linen down to the local launderette.

She came most days. She knitted, read magazines about love in hot climates, answered the phone when I was out. A widow, and childless, it seemed I was all she had.

Which wasn't much. It was hardly anything. But she was proud of me. My athletic and rugby medals adorned her mantelpiece, and she polished them relentlessly.

We chatted a while. She brewed up on the small stove and we shared a couple of cigarettes, then I found myself alone in my office.

I let time drift. The sky darkened, grew black. The streetlights came on, threw shadows into the room. I tried to recapture the atmosphere that had so chilled this room earlier in the day, recall the voice of Mrs Richardson, so sure that Karen was dead.

So where was Karen?

I had little information to work with. I didn't know where Karen worked, had gathered only that she had no friends—which I found hard to reconcile. Pretty girls had lots of friends—didn't they?

Was it possible for her to be friendless?

I guessed it was, but also guessed it to be quite unusual.

So where was I to start?

If no friends—find acquaintances. Discover where she worked, talk to her workmates. And track her movements for last Thursday, the day she packed and left her flat.

I dragged my mind away from Karen. I twisted to gaze from the window. No beauty greeted my eyes, only the reality of an industrial town in the grip of Winter. Overcoated men and women hunched into the rain, feet moving quickly, home to meals and television, the pub. A string of buildings, drab and grim, soot stained brick and mortar.

I sighed, feeling content, then the door opened and I was plunged into a dark pit. The visitor slammed the door, flopped on the divan, pulled off his shoes, and toasted his toes on the gas fire.

Seth Towers was an ugly rat-faced

19

individual of little charm; straight from the day shift, stinking of oil and compo, and making me nauseous.

I'd worked at his side for five years, straight from the Employment to him; five long, mind bending years at the Motor Works. He screwed on the nuts, and I tightened the buggers down. Eight hundred times a day we did that, for five years. Bad memories. The alarm clanging at six, the first fag, the first coffee, the one-mile trudge in the wind and rain, the newsagent's, the clock, the personalised white card with my own little number that I stuffed into it, clang. I was here, the time confirmed in its own little box. I hated that bloody clock.

When the redundancy money was offered I snatched their hands off. I rented this place. And here I was—a private detective. Most of my business concerned tracking down bad debtors. Some I found, some I didn't. I made no attempt to collect, I wasn't licensed. I passed on the information and let somebody else do the collecting. Maybe I have scruples, or maybe I lack the bottle, or maybe I realise that if I heard the old sob stories again I'd simply walk away and bury my head in the sand. I'm good at that.

Sometimes I work behind the bar at The Forger. Sometimes I work as a bouncer. Sometimes I find work as a casual labourer. It puts food on my table and clothes on my back.

It makes me an independent man.

Now, I glanced across to Seth and yawned to convey my boredom. It had no effect. He stretched out, contented, yapping away. He was nattering on about the wages snatch at the Motor Works. He was full of theories, each more bizarre than the last; Mafia, IRA, PLO, Billy Barber, the shifty and unpopular foreman on the production line who had recently bought a new car.

Finally, he glanced at his watch, and pushed off. I leaned back, dreamed my little dreams until it was time for me to leave.

*   *   *

I was a little startled by Val Spencer.

She was around forty, which made her some fifteen years older than her husband Ian. She was tall, and probably attractive in an angular way, though not to my taste. Her voice was brisk but not unpleasant. I had the idea she had once been the more than efficient secretary to some high-powered executive. She entertained me in the same office her husband had earlier in the day. I sat in the same chair. We had talked for some time.

'All right, I will go through it for you,' she was saying. 'Karen was seventeen at the time of the rape, which was a particularly savage one by any standards. The man was caught, convicted, and sentenced. Karen gave

21

evidence. It was a traumatic experience for her—the police questioning, the trial.'

She sighed. She examined her fingernails for a time. Then, reluctantly, she began to talk again. It was obvious she found it deeply painful.

'The Richardsons didn't go into details with you, so it seems that I shall have to. Karen became pregnant as a result of the rape.' I drew breath, and she noticed. 'Yes, another blow. And for a reason no one could fathom, Karen stubbornly insisted on bearing the child. Her parents objected, as did the doctors. A great deal of pressure was brought to bear on the girl. In the end she surrendered to it. The pregnancy was terminated. Karen was on the verge of a mental breakdown. She blamed her father. She found it hard to speak to him, almost unbearable to be in his presence.'

She paused. I didn't question her. I let her move at her own pace.

'My parents and the Richardsons were friends,' she went on. 'When Karen was born I became the unofficial baby minder. She was chronically shy, and made no friends of her own age. She preferred the company of older people. The Richardsons were well advanced into middle-age when she was born. She was their miracle child. They doted on her, especially the father. He denied her nothing— until he denied her that child. So Mrs Richardson thought a change of environment might help. I agreed. A promotion in my work had brought me north. I met Ian and married him. So Karen came here.'

'Did the Richardsons visit her?' I asked.

'From time to time. Mr Richardson stayed outside in the car. Karen sometimes spoke to her mother on the phone.'

I brought my mind back to more recent events. 'Karen told you she was leaving here?'

'Yes.' She shifted in her seat. 'Last Thursday evening. She said she was leaving for a while, possibly permanently.' I asked about the time. 'Around seven. I saw her in the hall when she came in.'

'Did she explain why she was leaving, where she intended to make for?'

'No.' Val shook her head. 'Probably she meant to, but the telephone chose that moment to ring.'

'And you didn't actually see her leave?'

'No. But I heard her come down the stairs around eight o'clock, possibly a little earlier.'

'But you didn't know she had left until next morning?'

'That is correct. Mrs Richardson telephoned around seven last Friday morning. She was distraught. She kept repeating that Karen was dead. She had had some kind of vision. I went upstairs and knocked on Karen's door. There was no response so I let myself in with the spare key she keeps with me. Her holdall was missing and most of the drawers cleared. Her bed had not been slept in. I went back to the telephone and told Mrs Richardson that Karen had left, presumably when I heard her leave the house the night before.'

'But when you spoke to Karen in the hall she didn't actually say she was leaving that evening?'

'No,' Val answered. 'I had presumed she meant in the coming days. And as I said, the telephone chose that moment to ring.'

I asked if it wasn't strange that Karen didn't pop in to say goodbye.

'Not really.' Val frowned. 'She was often thoughtless, very wrapped up in herself. She has been away before. Three, possibly four times.'

My ears pricked. I leaned forward.

'But she was never gone for more than a couple of days,' Val said quickly. 'On one of those occasions she forgot to mention that she'd be away.'

'Where did she go?' I asked. 'Who with?'

'I have no idea,' she answered.

More questions from me, answers from Val. She knew of no friends that Karen might be staying with. She wasn't surprised that Karen hadn't got in touch with her parents. I asked if Karen had seemed troubled lately.

'No more than usual.' Val's shrug was reflective. 'A little jumpy perhaps, thinner. But she had been like that for some weeks.' My eyebrows rose in question. She sighed. 'Karen had ceased to confide in me, and that is the truth. I'm head of department now. I also handle the paperwork for Ian. Karen resented that I had so little time to spare on her.' She paused. 'And you needed time with Karen. It was always a case of question and answer, and could be very tiresome.'

I asked how Karen had spent last Thursday. Val shrugged. She had seen and heard Karen only on the two occasions she had mentioned. She gave me a list of places where Karen had worked, those she could remember. It seemed Karen changed jobs often.

She took me upstairs to see Karen's flat.

The living room was furnished simply, everything neat and spotless. A few cans in the kitchen cupboard, little else. The bedroom was as featureless as any modern hotel room. I guessed there was little of Karen to be found here. I asked if she spent much time in the flat.

'A great deal,' Val said, leaning on the door with her arms folded as we stood in the living room. 'But it wasn't always as you see now. She had a TV, record player, lots of little gadgets she liked to toy with. She made it quite cosy.'

'Are you saying she carted all that lot away with her?' I asked.

'No,' Val replied. 'She sold them over a period of weeks.'

I couldn't keep the bewilderment from my

voice. 'Why?'

'I have no idea. I asked—but she refused to answer.'

'Presumably she needed the money?' I offered.

'Presumably. Though I can't think why.' Val chewed her lip. 'I know her parents pay the rent on this place. And Karen was never out of work for long, and hardly a big spender on food and clothes.'

She gestured me to the bedroom where she pulled open a drawer.

Dozens of sketches, different sizes; faces, landscapes, almost a travelogue of this town. They were good, and I commented on it.

'Yes, they are.' Val smiled. She seemed very pleased. 'She had a good eye.'

I flicked through the sketches. I recognised the scenes. The Waterloo arcade, the town centre, the park, the interior of a pub I knew. There were several nudes and it was easy to guess where they had been drawn. There were scenes from the Lake District. I recognised Windermere, the boats, the trees in the background.

I examined the portraits. There were several of the same man; a broad face, moustache and beard, lips turned back in a sneer, eyes menacing. In one there was a garage in the background and he wore overalls. All he lacked was a pair of horns to make him truly evil. I pointed him out to Val. She shuddered.

26

'I don't know who he is, and I certainly wouldn't like to meet him in the dark.'

I didn't blame her. I asked if the man could be Karen's boyfriend.

'Unlikely, knowing Karen.' Val had thawed completely. There was a touch of humour in her voice. I found I liked her. She went on, 'And the way she sketched him I'd say he was a character from a nightmare.'

We were leaving when I stopped in my tracks. The girl hovered in the doorway. She only smiled when she saw Val over my shoulder. She mumbled something about burglars. Val introduced us.

Her name was Jenny Gardener; small and cuddly, and breathlessly pretty. She had the flat across the landing. It was soon apparent that Val and she were friends. After some moments of explanation and small talk Val left us. I stared into her eyes and wondered if I was falling in love again.

CHAPTER FIVE

Tuesday; the alarm woke me at eight.

I stumbled from the divan. I lit the gas fire, dressed, and smoked a couple of cigarettes.

They did nothing for me. My head still throbbed, my throat stayed dry and choked.

I recalled the previous evening. Jenny

Gardener. She was twenty-four, and a typist in a solicitor's office in town.

Unfortunately, Jenny had not been a friend of Karen's. She knew little about the girl. She described Karen as remote and untouchable.

She hadn't seen Karen on the Thursday, but heard her twice. Once in the morning, around nine, and once in the evening, around eight. It didn't help me. I asked about the state of Karen's health.

'Oh, she wasn't blooming.' Jenny frowned. 'She had lost weight. And I know she was often sick because we share a bathroom. It began some five or six weeks ago roughly. I thought she might be pregnant, but dismissed that idea. She was sick all hours of the day and night. I mentioned that she looked ill and ought to see a doctor. She shrugged, but didn't respond.'

'Val said she probably left around eight last Thursday evening—is there a possibility she came back later? Did you hear her?'

'No. I didn't hear her, coming or going.' She shrugged. 'But I'm a heavy sleeper. And if Val says Karen didn't come back—then Karen didn't come back.'

I wasn't happy with my next question, but I put it all the same. 'Do you think Mrs Richardson might be right—that Karen might be dead?'

'Too creepy to contemplate.' She shivered. 'No, I don't believe in visions. I'm a realist.'

I took the plunge. I asked if I could give her

28

a ring later in the week. She smiled and held up her left hand. The diamond sparkled. I shrugged. It was the story of my life. Anyway, time pressed. I talked to the occupants on the first floor.

At the front there was a young married couple who had little information to impart. They hadn't seen Karen last Thursday, and didn't seem particularly interested that she might be missing. They were probably too besotted with each other to notice anything.

The tenant at the back proved slightly more interesting. She was an elderly lady, rather short-sighted and rather deaf, and happy to have company. She informed me she had sometimes chatted to Karen on the stairs, though somewhat vague as to the substance and content of these chats. I listened with half an ear and kept my eye on the time. I made my excuses and left the old woman to her TV.

Eight o'clock found me on duty at the door of a local pub that twice weekly ran pop concerts upstairs. I was the official bouncer, or steward as it said on my badge. Usually there wasn't much aggro, but last night had been an exception. Some slob had punched me in the stomach. I'd live, and he wouldn't chew meat for a month at least.

The concert over, a few beers under my belt, and I walked the streets for a while. It was an old habit that had lingered from my days in the police force. I had always preferred night duty. I loved the peace and the solitude.

Now, I yawned, forgot last night. I settled behind the desk and let my mind roam.

So where is Karen?

It was becoming a haunting refrain. And I still had no answer.

An enigma—that was Karen.

I went through the sketches again. I laid some aside. I made a mental list of the scenes depicted. I reckoned I was in for a long day.

Time to shift, time to sleuth, time to stick my nose where it didn't belong.

The rain still teemed down.

*   *   *

Business wasn't so hot.

The shop was drab, barely lit, floorboards creaked under my feet. In the corner a couple of young girls flicked through a rack of albums, giggled a lot, but showed no sign of buying.

The youngish woman with the silver streaks in her hair leaned on the counter and studied me. Possibly she reflected on her image of the private detective. If she did, I obviously didn't come up to expectations. I was just another bloke who might have stepped off any bus, perhaps even a little scruffier than most.

She sighed, rested her ample breasts on her folded arms. Her voice was deep and somewhat sexy.

'It must be about a year since she worked

here, love. Stayed two or three months. A pleasant enough girl. She didn't have a lot to say for herself. I knew no more about her when she left than when she started.' She paused. 'Always scratching on paper with her pen. Nice girl, not cheeky like some.'

I asked why Karen had left. She didn't know. She presumed Karen had simply grown bored with the job. I asked if Karen had friends who called at the shop.

'Not that I recall.' She pondered a few moments. 'I hoped a young face might bring the boys in. And it did to some extent. But she never nibbled, didn't seem interested in boys. She was an odd little thing. A shadow of a girl.'

A shadow? I was beginning to agree with that. I asked if she had seen Karen since the girl had left her employment.

'Once,' she replied. 'On the bus station if I remember right. Drawing in her notebook as usual. We said hello, but didn't converse.'

The two girls still giggled in the corner, but still gave no sign of buying as I left.

The next stop was a supermarket, with much the same result. The manager barely recalled her. Karen stayed only a few weeks. She made no friends.

So on I plodded. A launderette, a newsagent's. I learned little or nothing of Karen. I wandered onto the forecourt of a service station.

'There isn't a lot I can tell you, mate,' the

31

owner said. 'She worked here for a few months, on and off, mainly the evening shift. I'd no complaints. She did her job, was honest enough.'

'What was she like?' I asked.

'Quite good looking. Lovely little body. She gave the impression she was younger than she was. She had almost no conversation. She didn't make friends with the other girls. Seemed happiest when she was sketching. I never saw her again after she left, though I did hear someone mention having seen her working as an usherette. I liked the girl, but never got close.'

More questions. A lot of head shaking. Then his forehead creased into a frown.

'There was one strange incident.' He scratched his chin thoughtfully. 'She once threw one hell of a tantrum. She screamed until her face turned blue. She was serving a customer at the time. We wondered what was happening, if he'd touched her up or something. He was embarrassed as hell and sloped off. Anyway, when she calmed down she refused to explain what had happened. We never did figure it out.'

Karen had fractionally eased herself from the shadows in my mind.

*   *   *

It was no problem to find the cinema that had

employed Karen as an usherette. The town boasted just the one. The main doors were locked and I slipped down the alley at the side. I soon found the manager's office.

He was a young man in his middle twenties. He sprawled with his feet on the desk.

'I remember her, chum,' he said, toying with a sparse beard as if to stimulate it into growth. 'What is your interest in the girl?'

The question startled me. He was the first person to show anything but a fractional interest into why I was asking after Karen. So I gave him some of the truth. He listened, but his interest had quickly faded.

'I can't help you,' he said flatly. 'She worked here around last Spring. For about a month I reckon, then she left.'

It was all he had to say. I had outstayed my welcome, and he made it plain I was beginning to bore him.

*   *   *

The Waterloo arcade connected two main roads close to the town centre, and featured prominently in Karen's sketches. A century old, narrow, the walls of stained yellow and brown tiles; cool in Summer, even cooler in Winter, the roof a pyramid of dusty glass. Tightly packed stalls lined the walls leaving little space down the centre for pedestrians and customers, pressing them inwards, like

33

some mediaeval print.

'Yes, mate. Karen worked a few stalls round here.' The man was a little harassed, dealing with my questions and haggling with a woman over the price of a tea-set. 'I don't know much about her though. Try George Benson—the sweet stall at the bottom. Karen worked his stall more than any.'

The smirk I detected in his voice interested me, and the sickly grin he found impossible to hide. He hadn't finished.

'And now I come to think of it, I seem to remember George's daughter Sally mentioning Karen. Last Friday morning. Something about a van that nearly knocked her down the night before. Karen was in the van and Sally wanted to know who the driver was. But Sally yaps a lot. I wasn't paying particular attention. And all right, Karen was here last Thursday.'

The woman had wandered off. No money in the pocket. The man cursed under his breath.

'Mid-morning. Appeared around ten and stayed just over an hour. Jumpy as hell, dropped everything she touched. Then the cheeky monkey asked for money.' He shrugged thoughtfully. 'Though I have to admit that wasn't like her. She usually wouldn't say boo to a goose.'

Puzzled, I asked, 'How much did she want?'

'Forty quid.' The man laughed mirthlessly. 'I told her the forty quid would just about cover the breakages. I didn't even pay her for the hour she put in.'

'What sort of mood was she in?'

The man pondered on that. 'Like I said—jumpy. Mind you, she hasn't looked too good for a while, but never that bad. I advised her to see a doctor.'

Another potential customer drifted up. I was soon forgotten. I took his earlier advice.

George Benson was a plump, ruddy faced man in his middle fifties; all broad smiles and jolly banter until I mentioned Karen. He tensed, and his eyes hardened. For a time he tried to avoid my questions, but I pressed on.

'All right,' he said finally. 'I did see her last Thursday. But we didn't speak. She hovered about, then pushed off. I saw her leave the arcade and she didn't come back.'

'Did she ask you for money?' I put in.

'No. I said—we didn't speak.'

'But she often worked for you—you were friends?'

His eyes bored into mine. 'Just what the hell are you hinting at?'

I wasn't hinting at anything, but his attitude was surely confessing to something. I asked if Karen had seemed ill. He grunted something about Karen having been sick for some time. I took pains to explain who I was, and why I was here. He thawed a little, especially when he realised who I was. He was a rugby fan. I explained that the man on the crockery stall had told me that Benson's daughter had seen

Karen last Thursday night. It was news to him.

'Sally said nothing to me. Not that I'd expect her to.' His voice had soured, and it wasn't hard to guess that there was tension between father and daughter. 'Anyway, Sally's been away since Saturday. She'll be back tomorrow. You can call at the house if you want to see her. She rarely comes down here unless she wants something—beneath her dignity.'

I collected his address, and moved away.

*   *   *

This was a scene from one of Karen's sketches. I even found the bench she had sat on. The mound of grass, the gravel path, the KEEP OFF THE GRASS sign that everybody ignored, the circle of bushes, the ducks on the pond. One important feature was missing, so I waited on, fingers too numb to light a cigarette.

I pulled my coat tight, hands plunged deep inside my pockets, but the chill wind still blew through me. The park was barren, stark as a graveyard. No women pushed prams, no pensioners fed the ducks, no courting couples held hands.

And there was an itch between my shoulder blades, the uncomfortable notion that I was being watched. It had been there most of the morning, on and off. I told myself I was being jittery, though what I had to be jittery about I couldn't explain. I tried to shake the uneasy feeling aside.

Half an hour passed and my feet were blocks of ice. A middle-aged man came along the path, eyed me furtively, then quickened his pace. He probably had me marked down for a mugger. I certainly had that starved look.

At last!

I heard them before I saw them. Wild whoops, then suddenly they appeared over the mound, tapping a ball to each other and making out like they were playing for England. Two of them, both boys, something under ten years old. I watched them for a while before I whistled them over. They approached cautiously, but after a few unsteady moments we got along fine. With frozen fingers I extracted the photograph of Karen. They studied it.

They knew her. Her name was Karen and she came from Birmingham. She often sketched them. She wasn't too well. She shivered a lot even when the weather was warm. Only once had they seen her with another person. An old man. They touched hands. I guessed an old man to lads of this age was anything over forty. Still, the description was close to that of George Benson from the arcade, and that was something to file away at the back of my mind.

Karen had been in the park last Thursday,

around this time. She didn't speak to the boys. She appeared lost and distracted.

I kicked the ball around with them for five minutes to get the chill out of my bones, then drifted away.

Karen was sick.

A familiar theme with the people I'd spoken to. And I wasn't happy with what I was guessing to be the cause. Nausea, loss of weight, shivering, nerves. And I wondered how many jokers she had come into contact with over the past few weeks had thought along the same lines. Plenty, I guessed. Though no one I had spoken to had put those speculations into words.

*   *   *

I opened the door to the parlour of the Three Bells, and entered. I had been right. This was another scene from Karen's sketches.

Two elderly women seated in the corner studied my intrusion as if I'd fallen from outer space. Males were not welcome in this room. I ignored them. I allowed my eyes to settle on the only other occupant. She sat at a table in the centre of the room. I smiled.

Estimates of Pauline's age varied from thirty to sixty, and anywhere in that range could have been correct. She was a huge but gentle woman, whose head resembled a giant turnip. I knew her well, had arrested her more than once. A good natured alcoholic was Pauline, one of the dying breed; no fuss, no bother; an eccentric who enjoyed the odd night in a police cell, and the breakfast that came with it. She was never less than good humoured.

She was happy to see me, touchingly so. We bantered on old times, joked a lot. Then I pulled out the photograph of Karen.

'Ah.' She smiled, and her eyes almost disappeared in rolls of fat. I asked the questions and she was happy to answer. 'She came in here a lot—just to sketch, you know. She didn't drink. She said it made her poorly. She said you found lots of interesting faces in here, and nobody pestered you. Sometimes she sat with me, sometimes she sat in the corner. She didn't speak much. She was different from most kids you meet today.'

That was true enough. I asked if Karen had been in here last Thursday.

Pauline laughed. 'Oh, yes. She asked if I could lend her forty pounds. "Some hope," I told her.' Pauline went quiet. 'I liked her. If I'd had the money she'd have been welcome to it. But I didn't.' She took a sad sigh. 'She was in here twice that day. Came in at one and stayed about half an hour. Then she was back around six, stayed perhaps an hour this time. I asked if she had managed to get the money, but she shook her head. The poor girl was in quite a state.'

I asked what was wrong with her.

'Who knows? She didn't confide in me. I don't understand young people. Perhaps she was pregnant—I don't know. All she said was that she had been to the pictures.'

'Oh.' I leaned forward. 'And?'

'Just that. She'd been to the pictures.'

'That day—the Thursday?'

'That's right.'

To see the manager of the cinema? I wondered. It might be worth paying another visit on that young man.

I bought Pauline a drink, and asked a few questions around the pub, but learned nothing.

CHAPTER SIX

Bloody hell!

This took me back to my schooldays, and that didn't exactly fill me with joy.

I was in the local Technical College; built in the sixties when there was still plenty of money to be tossed around on flashy enterprises. A giant concrete and glass monolith, four storeys high.

I tramped the deserted corridor. Hollow voices reached me from behind the closed doors of the classrooms, the echo of my own feet swung back to me, my reflection marching along in tune as it was thrown back from the glass wall and the black void of the night beyond.

I shivered. I stopped, turned. Nothing behind me, not so much as a shadow. I shook my head ruefully. I was getting paranoid. I continued on my way.

I checked the numbers, found the one I wanted, and quietly slipped inside. A few inquisitive faces turned my way, the rest remained indifferent.

And success. A triumph for my intellect. This was the room from Karen's sketches.

There must have been a dozen of them, all chalking away like budding Rembrandts, the youngest in her teens, the eldest around seventy, struggling with stiff fingers.

I eyed the model in the far corner where a screen had been placed against the window to protect her dignity from the gaze of perverted owls. I had seen her before, sketched in carbon on white paper. Karen had caught her exactly. Pushing thirty, good breasts and legs, a fetching face that showed little emotion.

'Can I help you?'

I glanced up.

He towered over me. At least six foot six and in the region of eighteen stone. The scar on his nose and the badge on his blazer told me how he spent his Saturday afternoons. I didn't doubt he was a mean bugger in the maul or ruck. He smiled. His voice was as big and friendly as his face.

41

'You're Frankie Conroy,' he boomed. 'I once played against you before you turned pro.'

We shook hands. We both knew I didn't recognise him, but neither of us said so. We chatted for a while, then I explained why I was here.

'That's right,' he said. 'Karen is one of my pupils. Tonight is the first time she's missed this term.'

Nightschool, one night a week. Tuesdays, luckily for me. But still, I had the sinking feeling I'd come up against another brick wall.

'Quite a talented girl,' he went on. 'Though not brilliant, by any stretch of the imagination. She would never make a living at it. But she was improving all the time.' He shrugged. 'So who can say.'

I asked if he could give me an insight into her personality, expecting the usual reply, and getting it.

'No.' He seemed a touch bewildered. 'Pleasant enough to speak to, when she chose to speak, which wasn't often. I have to admit I know next to nothing about the girl.' I asked about her health. 'Come to think of it, she has seemed a little off-colour lately.' I asked if she had made friends in the class, and was greeted with the expected shake of the head. 'No. I'm more or less certain she didn't. But you are free to ask around.'

I did, and learned nothing. We were at the

door when he began to scratch his head.

'One thing that might interest you,' he said quietly. 'It happened some weeks back. I saw Karen getting out of a car outside this building. I caught a glimpse of the driver as she walked away. His face was in shadow, but I saw his eyes. They devoured her, like a starving dog eyeing a meaty bone on the other side of a barbed wire fence. Maybe I'm being a bit melodramatic—but you know the sort of look I mean.'

I guessed I did. And at least this was something. I asked if he could describe the man.

'No.' His head shook. 'It was a mere glimpse at some distance. I thought little of it at the time. You brought it back to mind.'

'The car?' I asked.

'Sorry.' Another shrug. 'I didn't notice. A medium sized car. I couldn't even give you the colour.'

'The age of the man?'

'Young—certainly. Possibly clean shaven—yes, definitely clean shaven.'

Just another snippet of information to be filed away. He wished me luck in my search for Karen, and I thanked him for his time.

*   *   *

I marched through the foyer, ignored the faces that turned my way, leapt the short flight of steps, and entered the office without knocking. I leaned with my back against the door.

'What game are you on, chum!'

The manager of the cinema was on his feet, coming quickly around the desk. He came to a sudden halt in front of me. He matched my height but I could take him with one hand tied behind my back, and he knew it.

'You can scream, my friend,' I hissed. 'And somebody will come. But I'll be back—you can bet on that. You lied. Karen was here last Thursday.' Now the lies began to trip off my tongue. 'She was seen. Want me to give you the exact time!'

'I knew the girl meant trouble.' He shrugged, pulled a face. He returned to sprawl in his chair. His voice retained some of its cockiness. 'What do you want to know?'

'Why she came here—why you lied to me.'

'She came for money.' He eyed me warily as I took a seat. 'She wanted forty pounds.'

That again. 'Why come to you?'

'I'll explain.' He startled me by pulling his shirt off his shoulder and pointing to a dark circular scar. 'She did that.'

'The hell she did.' I whistled softly. Little Karen had something of the tigress in her. I recalled the owner of the service station recounting the tantrum Karen had once thrown on the forecourt. 'How? Why?'

'I haven't much time, chum, so let's make it snappy.' He glanced at his watch meaningfully.

'I was once foolish enough to make a play at her. We were both single—so why not? I swear I only put my arm round her and gave her a bit of a squeeze to let her know I was interested. She blew! Hell! How she blew!' He motioned to the scar again. 'I had a hell of a time explaining to the doctor how I'd tumbled head over arse and finished with a pencil sticking out of my shoulder like a bloody arrow.'

'Did you strike her?' I asked.

'No. Course not.' He seemed to find my question odd. 'I was screaming and she was crying. Somebody came crashing through the door to see what the commotion was about, and I was soon on my way to the hospital. She turned up next day and asked for her cards. I was happy to see her go.'

'That hardly explains why she came to you for money,' I pointed out.

'It might.' He sat up and leaned forward. 'It was weird. Last Thursday afternoon. It was the first time I'd clapped eyes on her since she left. She was thinner, and rougher. She tried to touch me for the forty quid I mentioned. I told her to leave. Then she started to strip. I couldn't believe it. She scared the hell out of me. She was saying I could do anything I liked for forty quid. I didn't like. I told her to button up her coat—and quick.' He leaned back again. 'She came to me because she probably thought I was still hot for her. She was desperate.'

45

He was right there. 'So why did you lie to me?'

'Chum,' he said quietly. 'I've been around. I know a junkie when I see one. I didn't want to get mixed up in anything.'

At last! I sighed inwardly. Somebody had turned my thoughts into words. Karen was a drug addict. I asked more questions. He had never given Karen a ride in his car. He drove an old MGB. I left it there.

* * *

The Forger was more crowded than usual; a lot of young people packed tight around the bar. I played a game of darts. I tried to join in the banter, but nothing worked. I was still depressed. I moved to one of the small rooms at the back and settled down with a glass in my hand. I stared into the blazing fire. My mind drifted to Karen.

Karen was a junkie—crudely put. Not confirmed, but ninety-nine percent certain.

So who supplied her with the stuff?

Hell! That was going to be a hard one. And if I never found Karen—I decided I'd find the bastard who supplied her.

Most people think the drug problem is confined to the big cities. Well, they were wrong. It was everywhere, everywhere that young people congregated, where there was a pound to be made, even in a backwater such as this. There was always the pusher; sliding from hole to hole like the greasy snake he was; an eye for the vulnerable, the lonely. I'd seen it. I'd met it. And the problem was on the increase.

I got angry. Another pint slipped away, then another. An old refrain entered my head.

Was Karen friendless?

No, that couldn't be. There had to be somebody she confided in. A man, a woman. The guy who dropped her off for art class, the guy with the hungry eyes? The old guy she held hands with in the park, who might possibly be George Benson from the arcade? And what about the guy she sketched so often? Maybe he supplied her with drugs. Why had she drawn him with such a wicked face? There was no way he could look like that. I decided to concentrate on him for a while— number one priority. The overalls were the clue.

Closing time had come and gone. I stayed behind and helped clear up. I chatted with the landlord for a while. He kept yawning, too tired to listen to my problems tonight. I drifted out.

I took to the alleys; not drunk, but definitely groggy. I walked the night again. The wind and rain whipped around me, tossed my hair in different directions. It felt good.

The dark cloaked me, but I knew I wasn't alone. There was always something. Animal or human, a twitch of a curtain, a white face in the shadows, scavenging dogs. I avoided the lighted streets.

My square mile. Even when they inflicted a Panda car on me I tucked it away and found an excuse to walk, plod the alleys and the backs, nose out sin and corruption, boots slick with rain and mud. I saw the outline of the old mill and the giant chimney stack that had once pumped filth into the sky. Abandoned, a monument to the past. Plenty of schools and eerie schoolyards, plenty of broken windows. There was a predominance of churches and chapels; Catholic, Church of England, Baptist, Methodist; you found them all huddled around here, their edifices grim in the night. I plodded on.

They were around somewhere—the night people. The dog walkers, the insomniacs, the lonely, the kinks, my pal the transvestite who whipped on his wife's frock and did a quick circuit of the block every night, Rita the ancient whore, imprisoned under ten coats of varnish, hovering and ready to pounce on the first drunk who stumbled her way.

I stepped into a dark doorway to light a cigarette. I never struck the match. Suddenly, the hairs on the back of my neck had bristled.

I heard feet whispering closer. My fists bunched. I stepped out.

No fists flying. No punch-up. I almost burst into tears.

She was well over sixty. Her face was hidden under the wide brim of her hat. I could just make out her chin and mouth. She didn't seem the least bit perturbed, which made the situation even more bizarre.

'You shouldn't do that, young man,' she admonished in a prim voice. 'You are much too old to play such silly pranks. You frightened me.'

I watched her dissolve into the night. She had been about as frightened as a Chieftain tank coming up against a water pistol. But she had lightened my mood. I whistled happily as I walked on. I loved the night, and the characters who inhabited it. Nothing to fear in the night, only what you can't handle with your bare fists.

I turned into the dark courtyard and climbed the wooden stairs. I had sobered, suddenly grim again, thoughts returning to Karen.

The warmth hit me as soon as I opened the door. A grim, rectangular, barrack-like room confronted me. Hard chairs in lines faced a dark stage where I'd often watched the band practise while I dreamed away a few hours in contented bliss. The plaster walls were painted an ugly shade of yellow and orange.

Not many in tonight. An old man in the middle of the room, chin drooped to his chest in repose. In front of him a younger man lay stretched along a row of chairs. His head lay in the crook of his arm. He was possibly asleep, though probably not. Another man sat on a chair near the wall, clasping a plastic bag to his chest as if it contained all he owned, and most likely did. He appeared infinitely old, but I guessed his age to be close to mine. He mumbled under his breath, hummed a strange dirge. Jesus wanted him for a sunbeam. And sweet Jesus, I begged humbly, please take him.

I took a seat at the back, swamped by the stink of human sweat and misery, disinfectant and despair. I lit a cigarette, let the minutes drift.

I heard the solid clump of feet on wooden boards, the squeak of the chair beside me, the smell of serge. A mug was pushed into my hand and I wrapped my fingers around it to draw in the warmth. I raised it to my lips and let the hot sweetness slide down my throat. I didn't look to the newcomer, nor did we converse for some time.

Finally, he asked, 'How many, Frank?'

'Four, five, six,' I mumbled. 'I wasn't counting. I'm sober enough.'

'Good. How's the knee?'

'Okay—till you mentioned it.'

Now I glanced up to him. He had the worn and caring countenance of the long distance sufferer. He was over sixty, with the energy and drive of a man half his age. His hair was steely grey where it peeked from under his cap. Major Seddon was an old pal from way back, a substitute father in many respects. King of the Salvation Army we called him when I was a kid. In those days my great ambition was to play trombone in the band. But I could never wear that uniform. I could never be one of God's army. I didn't believe.

'Problems?' he asked.

'A puzzle,' I said quietly. 'A young woman is missing. Nineteen, but in most ways a lot younger. Her mother hired me to find her. In the morning I want you to check, see if your people have any knowledge of her. She just might have stumbled into one of your shelters.'

He nodded solemnly.

I began to recount the story, starting from the moment the Richardsons entered my office. He listened carefully, as I knew he would. The tea was gone, and I lit another cigarette.

'And you believe the mother?' Major Seddon asked. 'You think she experienced the death of her daughter?'

'Not really,' I said, unconvinced. It was hard to explain, even to this man, how concerned I was for Karen—a girl I had never met. 'Do you think it possible?'

'I didn't meet the mother,' he said mildly. 'She obviously had some kind of psychic experience. It is possible. Yes, there is a part of the human mind that remains a mystery to us. Much stranger events have occurred. And the girl is missing.'

'That she is.' I twisted restlessly. 'I've traced people before, but this is different. There is usually a friend, a relative, something in the past to use as a lead. But here there is nothing. No friends, just a mother and father in Birmingham.'

He sighed, examined his hands. 'Have you approached the Samaritans?'

Oh, hell! I hadn't thought of that. I mumbled something about Karen not being suicidal.

'I wasn't thinking of suicide.' A weary smile creased his mouth. 'You don't need to be contemplating suicide to call the Samaritans. It is a plea for help. In trouble, any trouble, and they are there, a final desperate chance.' He paused. 'I'll enquire for you myself. Simpler that way. It will save explanations.'

I nodded, thanked him.

'I'm always here, Frank,' he said.

And that was good to know. I stood, shook his hand.

Outside, the rain had eased, the wind less biting. I pondered on where to spend the night. Mrs Harker's was on the other side of town. Too far to walk, and I was in no condition to drive.

I shook my head free of the phantoms that had begun to haunt me, and trudged back to the empty office, and a cold and uninviting bed.

CHAPTER SEVEN

Morning. Wednesday. The view from my office bleak. It still rained; now a damp grey drizzle.

I studied the sketches of the man with the wicked face, the evil one of Karen's imagination. I tucked the least draconian of the sketches into my pocket, and stepped once more into the wet and cold.

Lots of garages, big and small. I showed the sketch to office girls and men in overalls; some showed mild interest, some dismissed me with a bare shake of the head.

But I guess I was lucky. It was at garage number nine that I struck gold, and it wasn't yet noon. A medium sized repair shop that employed perhaps a dozen men and a couple of office staff. The chargehand glanced at the sketch and nodded.

'Eddie Morgan,' he said flatly.

'Is he around?' I asked quickly, too quickly.

His eyebrows rose, and I detected a smirk. If I was right, he had just marked me down as a jealous husband.

'No,' he answered. 'I fired him. Must be going on two months back.'

I tried to cover my disappointment. I asked why he had fired Morgan.

'He worked too many fiddles. I overlook the odd one as part of the game, but he overstepped the mark. He tapped the customers for homework, then had the nerve to book down the parts he used to us.'

I asked if the police had been brought in. He shook his head. Not worth it. Chalk another up to experience. I asked what Morgan was like.

'A good mechanic.' The man let out a long breath. 'But not popular. Thought he was something special. He wasn't. A good looking lad though. The girls liked him.'

I asked if he knew where Morgan went from here.

'Yes.' He nodded. 'A ragbag outfit on Cumberland Road. Just Morgan's style. S and G Repairs.' I was about to leave when he stopped me. His face wore a smile. 'Whoever drew the sketch didn't seem to like him. The artist worked here for a while I reckon— Karen?'

That took my breath away. Val Spencer hadn't mentioned that Karen worked here. Though she had pointed out that the list she gave me wasn't extensive. I asked the man if we were talking about Karen Richardson.

'That's the one.' His smile broadened. 'Odd little thing. Fetching enough, but definitely something odd about her. Always sketching. Made the tea, answered the phone, did her work, went home.'

I asked if Karen had been friendly with Morgan. He took his time answering.

'Now you mention it—friendlier than most, despite the sketch you're carrying. Though I doubt if it got him anywhere. I shouldn't think he made her.'

I asked how long Karen had worked here, and when.

'Four or five weeks. Left a fortnight after Morgan. Their employment overlapped.'

I asked why she left. He reckoned she simply got bored, or ran out of things to sketch.

I asked about the state of her health when she worked here. That puzzled him. He frowned.

'We don't ask for a doctor's certificate, but she looked healthy enough to me. What's this all about?'

I gave him a little of the story. I asked if he had seen Karen since she left and he shook his head. He asked around the garage for me, but the answer was the same—nothing.

But now I had a name to work with. Eddie Morgan. And the deterioration in Karen's health had begun some weeks back—possibly about the time she met Morgan. I was making progress at last.

*   *   *

S and G Repairs didn't look like a ragbag outfit to me; a hive of activity and noise. Cars on ramps, the hiss of a welding torch, the roar of pop music from a radio.

I found the co-owner, a young man who went under the name of Stan. He wiped the oil from his hands with a rag and asked what he could do for me.

Innocently, I asked if Eddie Morgan was around.

Hostility flashed in his eyes. His voice matched. 'And what business would you have with him, old pal?'

I wasn't his old pal, or anyone else's for that matter. I kept my voice cool. I told him Eddie owed me money and I was here to collect.

'Then you can collect elsewhere,' he snapped. 'He slung his hook last Friday. Collected his cards and shoved off. Two lads down with flu and that bastard walks out on us.'

I asked why Morgan had left. The young man was happy to talk. He was getting something off his chest.

'He didn't say. He acted oddly all that day, right from the first. Suppressed ecstasy you might say, like a kid living on his first promise. Then he makes a phone call and suddenly he has toothache, has to take himself off to the dentist. So he went. Next thing I know he's back, almost shitting himself, white as a sheet. He demands his cards and wages. We argue, then I decide what the hell, better off without him. That was the last time I clapped eyes on him.'

I found this fascinating. I pressed. 'So he's excited in the morning, then his mood does a somersault. So what happened?'

'Search me.' The young man shrugged. 'Something put the wind up him—and it wasn't the dentist.'

I asked for Morgan's address and he disappeared into a tiny office. He returned and shoved a crumpled slip of paper into my hand. 'If you find him, old pal, stick one on him for me.'

I nodded. I took out the photograph of Karen and asked if she ever came to the garage.

'Just the once. The day before Morgan cleared out. It would be the Thursday.'

My luck was changing, and fast. I pressed for details. He didn't need to ponder on his answers.

'I can give you the exact time. From half past eleven in the morning till one in the afternoon. She asked if Morgan was around. He was out on a job so she waited.' He pointed to an oil drum near the sliding door. 'There she sat. Knees pressed together like a schoolgirl. I remember thinking that Morgan was pulling them young. She couldn't have been much over sixteen.'

I asked if anybody had talked to her.

'No,' he replied. 'She seemed to be in a world of her own. Then Morgan came back. He wasn't happy to see her. They argued. Or

57

rather, he shouted and she cringed. Then he was pushing her through the door. I heard him shout something like, "No money—no goodies." I don't know what he meant.'

I guessed I did. I was taking a chance now. 'Did Morgan ever mention drugs? Did he know where to lay his hands on the hard stuff?'

The young man's eyes held mine. 'Who the hell are you?'

I told him, mostly the truth. He listened. He lit the stub of a fat cigar, squinting as the smoke curled into his eyes.

'Sorry, I can't help.' His tone had softened. 'Morgan never mentioned drugs to me. He smoked grass. He used to brag about it. But as for the hard stuff—' He shrugged, studied me a bit longer. 'Is that what the bogies wanted him for?'

Bewildered, my jaw slackened. 'Bogies?'

'The police. CID. Late afternoon, or early evening. The Friday he jacked. They wanted Morgan.'

'Why?'

'No idea. I thought he'd been nicking. If you hadn't come clean with me I wouldn't have mentioned them. And this talk of drugs made me think that might be the reason he scarpered so quick.'

I asked if these policemen had identified themselves. He scratched his head.

'No. Come to think of it—they didn't. They just acted like bogies. They asked about the girl too. I told them the same as you.'

I asked for a description of the two men.

'Both big guys, as you'd expect bogies to be. One had a moustache and beard, a great bush of curly black hair. The other was lighter skinned, kept his mouth shut, didn't utter a word.'

More questions, but he had nothing to add, nor had the other lads in the garage.

*   *   *

The section of town where Eddie Morgan lived was a jumble of old and towering town houses that showed the stains of decay and grime after a century of neglect; now chopped into a multitude of flats.

I thumbed the bell by the door and it opened warily. It took a little explaining before I was allowed inside.

She was tall, heavy breasted, skin very white under a thick thatch of raven hair, as if she never glimpsed the light of day. I put her age at twenty-eight, and her description as moderately striking. I asked if she was Mrs Morgan. She laughed without humour, sat on the sofa and crossed her legs in a swift movement.

'Irene Downes is the name,' she said in a voice that shaded on the husky. 'I am what the papers refer to as a common law wife—and in my case—very common.'

59

If that was intended as a joke it didn't strike me as humorous. She examined me with dark eyes and I twisted uncomfortably, partly because she seemed to be exploring my brain, partly because of the generous amount of thigh she was putting on view.

'Do you make a living at this game?' she asked.

'I survive.' I left her legs and concentrated on her eyes. 'Plenty of stones to be upturned, plenty of worms to be exposed to daylight—so where is Eddie?'

'You tell me.' Her voice turned sour. 'He showed up here last Friday afternoon. He packed his bags, got into his car, and cleared out. I haven't seen or heard from him since.'

I didn't know whether to believe her or not. Though there was that bitter ring of truth in her voice. I asked where Eddie had gone.

The reply was short and sweet. 'He didn't say.'

'Yet you lived with him.'

'Clever lad. I bet the villains go weak at the knees when they find you sniffing along their trail.' A harsh laugh greeted her own wit. 'But true. We lived together for almost a year. I'm left to wonder if we still do—or if he's gone for good.'

'So where is he?' I pressed. She raised weary eyes to the ceiling. They soon snapped back to me when I asked, 'Did he leave with Karen Richardson?'

60

'That's ridiculous!' Her contempt showered over me. 'She couldn't satisfy Eddie for more than a minute.'

I couldn't hide the gloating pleasure from my voice. 'So Karen was his new girlfriend?'

'You are a pathetic little man!' She lit a cigarette with the sudden flare of a lighter, blew smoke through her nostrils in twin streams. 'He brought her back here a few times. She was nothing.'

Though enough to get under Irene Downes's skin. I asked how she had got along with Karen.

'Fine!' she snapped. 'She was house trained.'

'Jealous?' I goaded.

'Funny,' she mimicked.

I went for the throat. 'What type of shit was Eddie pumping into her arm—heroin?'

Hell! That made her sit up. She ground out the cigarette. Heavy breasts strained against cotton as she took in air.

'I know nothing about that!' she hissed. 'Eddie didn't meddle in drugs. If she was into anything—she didn't get it from Eddie.'

'You and Eddie smoked grass,' I said evenly. 'He bragged about it.'

'The occasional joint,' she responded. 'Who doesn't?'

Me, for one, and fifty million others who could hardly scrape up the price of a packet of Woodbines. I decided I would get nowhere with this one. Hard as steel, with a heart to match. Then she surprised me.

'You might find him in Bolton. That's where he originates from. He has a brother.' She snapped out an address. 'And if you find him, you might let me know.'

I wasn't her errand boy. 'Pick up a phone, or hop on a bus.'

'I crawl to no man! If he wants to come back—he crawls to me!'

Like hell! She'd have him back, crawling or otherwise. But she had pride. At least I admired that streak in her. I made it to the door and turned.

'Late Friday afternoon, after Eddie left, did anybody come around here asking questions? Two men, big, detectives maybe?'

'No!' Short and snappy.

'The day before, Thursday, did Karen come looking for Eddie?'

I thought I saw a hint of fear register in her eyes, but her reply was again terse.

'No!'

I slammed out, but knew I'd be back.

*   *   *

At last!

The silly trollop finally decided to drop the phone into the cradle. She even had the cheek to glare at me as she left the box.

I dialled, waited, then punched home the

coin.

'Sergeant Bell, urgent. This is Frank Conroy.'

It was several minutes and another coin in the slot before he came on.

'What game are you on, Kevin, you two-faced bastard!' I bawled. 'You said you'd made no enquiries about Karen Richardson!'

'Hold on!' His tone was the equal of mine. 'What the devil are you whining about now, Frankie?'

The bluff had been called. I described the two men who had visited the garage looking for Eddie Morgan and Karen. He didn't recognise the descriptions.

'Somebody is having you on,' he said quietly. 'Last Friday I hadn't even heard of Karen Richardson. Her parents called here on Sunday. And we have no interest in Karen Richardson, not last Friday, not today.' He paused. 'And you say these men claimed to be police officers?'

'Not exactly,' I admitted. 'But they gave that impression. So they must have smelled right.' I did some quick thinking. 'Have you heard of an Eddie Morgan?'

'Rings a faint bell. I can check.'

I considered a moment. 'No. Maybe later. I'm tracking him down. I'll get the answers from him with a bit of luck.'

*   *   *

63

It was on my way, so I decided to drop in.

Ian Spencer sat on a stool in front of a drawing board in his studio at the back of the house. He appeared to welcome the interruption. He listened patiently to my story.

'Ravenous eyes that peer from the shadows,' he said when I had finished. He made no attempt to conceal his smile. 'It sounds to me as if someone has a rather vivid and wild imagination, Frank.'

'It does when you put it that way,' I confessed. 'But in my opinion the teacher was a down-to-earth bloke. So you never drove her to night class?'

'No,' he said. 'I don't think she was ever in my car. And I didn't even know she attended art class. Did the description fit me?'

'No. There was no description, excepting that the man was young and clean shaven— apart from the bit about the eyes.'

'Sorry—I can't help.' He shrugged.

I let him get back to his work. I'd have liked a word with Val, but she was working and wouldn't be back until quite late.

I noticed the car slide into the traffic behind as soon as I pulled from the kerb. A dark blue Rover, two occupants. Their faces were hidden behind a dusky windscreen. It took the same road, kept its distance. I slowed, it slowed. My heart beat a little faster. For two miles we played out this strange mating tango. Then the car signalled right, and was gone from my mirror. I smiled, and a tremor of relief ran through me. I cursed my edginess. I soon forgot about the car.

CHAPTER EIGHT

David Morgan bore a vague similarity of features to the sketches Karen had made of his brother. But he was younger, clear eyes that met the world head-on. His attitude had been guarded when I asked if Eddie was home. Five minutes later we retired to the pub at the corner of his street.

He asked bluntly, 'Are you the police?'

'Private.' I showed him a dog eared card. 'I'm tracing him in connection with a problem that has arisen.'

He didn't ask what problem. He took a deep breath and met my eyes. His voice was flat. 'You're too late, mate. My brother is dead.'

I felt my spine weaken. Another lead to Karen blown. I was suddenly mad with Eddie Morgan for getting himself killed, ridiculously so under the circumstances. I asked about Eddie's death.

'Last Friday night,' he replied. 'Just after eleven. He was drunk. His car skidded and hit a tree. He died instantly. And that's about it.'

A tight knot of apprehension settled in my

stomach.

Was Eddie's death connected with his flight earlier that day—with Karen's disappearance? Why had he suddenly returned to Bolton? Who were the men searching for him? I began to question David, and he answered without hesitation.

'He appeared from the blue—Friday afternoon. Knocked on the door, and pushed inside.' I got the impression David hadn't been too happy about that. 'He was very agitated, which wasn't like Eddie. I asked if anything was wrong and he told me to mind my own business.' He shrugged. 'Which was fine with me.

'He didn't stay long. That was the last I saw of him. Early Saturday morning the police knocked me up with the news. We once shared the flat, and that was the address on his driving licence.'

I asked why Eddie had come to see him that day. This time he pondered on his reply.

'He was obviously in trouble. He'd been away a long time and lost touch. He wanted to know if I'd seen any of his old mates lately. He was looking for somebody who could connect him with a job in Birmingham, or London. He said he had to get out of the north for a while.'

'Did you help him?' I asked.

'No.' David drained his glass and stared into it thoughtfully. 'I never really mixed with Eddie's crowd. Oh, I knew who they were. I'd met them. But they were never my type. So—I couldn't help him. He also wanted money, which was probably the real reason he came to me. He got none.'

'So what did Eddie do?' I asked.

'He decided to make a tour of his old haunts, search out his old contacts.'

'Did anybody come looking for Eddie after he left?' I described Curly and Mute, as I had dubbed the ghostly pair. 'Maybe they claimed to be policemen.'

'Odd policemen.' David groaned, touched his stomach as though it hurt. 'But I did think they were CID at first. Eddie reappearing out of nowhere, then these two blokes knocking on the door, asking after him.'

'What did you tell them?'

'That I hadn't seen Eddie in months. Then one of the bleeders punched me in the stomach. I was on the floor. It was like something out of a bad movie.' He winced. His smile was grim. 'The quiet one started to clean his nails with a knife, and the other said I was a liar. They'd spoken to the lady in the flat below. She'd let Eddie through the front door earlier.'

'So you told these men where to find Eddie?'

A pained expression crossed his face, a shade of guilt. 'I wasn't about to let myself get carved up for Eddie—no way. I gave them the names of a few pubs. Anyway, I thought it unlikely they'd be able to track Eddie down—very unlikely.'

'Do you think they found him?' I asked.

'No. He wrapped his car around—' There was a touch of shock in his eyes. 'You don't believe—?'

'I don't know what to believe,' I said wearily. I showed him the photograph of Karen. He recognised her.

'I saw her just the one time. At Eddie's place. She was there, and the piece he lived with, Irene Downes. Christ! What an atmosphere! It made me want to puke. The girl squatted in the corner, legs pulled under her chin. Eddie said she was playing at being invisible—whatever that meant. The Downes piece sat staring at the television and didn't so much as blink or utter a word. I cleared out quick. I never called again.'

I asked if he had spoken to the girl.

'No,' he answered. 'She simply squatted there, eyes fixed on Eddie.'

I asked if Eddie meddled in drugs.

'Maybe.' He paused. 'The girl certainly appeared to be on something—and the way she watched Eddie—' He shrugged. 'I'd say it was possible.'

I asked if Eddie had a police record.

'He did a couple of years on probation for pinching cars when he was in his teens. Nothing since.'

'When the two men came looking for

Eddie—did they mention the girl—Karen?'

He nodded. 'They asked if she was with Eddie when he called. She wasn't.'

'When the police came to inform you of the accident—did you mention the two men to them?'

'No. I saw no point.'

I asked if Irene Downes knew what had happened to Eddie. He seemed puzzled.

'No. I only told the relatives. Should I have told her? Did Eddie mean anything to her?'

I shrugged and we shook hands.

I decided to have a few words with the lady who occupied the ground floor flat in the same building as David. She turned out to be very bright and chatty.

She remembered the two men who had called the previous Friday. Yes, they had been looking for Eddie Morgan. Eddie once lived in the flat above. Yes, they had asked about a girl. But Eddie had definitely been alone. Yes, she had glanced out of the window when she heard Eddie's car pull up. And yes, if Eddie had left a girl in the car while he came inside she would have noticed. There was positively no girl.

She pulled me into a room that smelled of furniture polish and cats and I was soon sitting down with a newspaper on my knee. It carried a sketchy account of Eddie Morgan's accident. He was the single occupant of the car. There was an interview with the old couple who had witnessed the accident, giving their address.

There was mention of another car, a large dark saloon. It wasn't much, but something I decided to check on.

*   *   *

The rain had eased, a spattering of stars flickering through the breaks in the clouds, but the temperature had dropped. I was parked on the wide circular road that swept around the town; the neat semi-detached houses spaced at regular intervals on either side. And I had found the spot where Eddie Morgan died.

Unlucky Eddie. He had contrived to hit the only tree in a hundred yards. It still bore the scars of the collision; but the tree would recover, Eddie wouldn't. The address of the witnesses was on the other side of the road.

I was soon inside the neat front room, comforted by the roaring fire and the glass in my hand.

Reliable witnesses? Well, who was I to judge? Were they to be discounted because of their age? Both were around the eightyish mark. Both wore glasses. The woman did most of the talking.

'We were returning from the club, around eleven. We were perhaps fifty yards away. The car that hit the tree seemed to be weaving about. Course, at the time we could really only see the lights. Then another car passed it. A big dark thing. It seemed to cut in front of the

70

other. The little car swerved and hit the tree. The horn blared because the driver must have fallen on it. A great racket it made. Lights went on all over the place and doors opened.'

I asked if the dark car had stopped.

'No,' she stated. 'It slowed for a second—then shot off. I suppose the driver didn't want to get involved.'

I asked if she had seen the face of the man who had driven the dark car, if there was more than one occupant.

She shook her head. And I believed her story. I had already leapt to the conclusion that Morgan had been deliberately run off the road, and I had more than a good idea that the dark car had contained two men—Curly and Mute. But whether they had meant to kill Morgan was another matter.

I was back in my car, heading home, mind turning. The sky had darkened again and the rain began to lash down. The hot air that pumped into the interior made me drowsy.

I was soon wide awake. The lights at first, hitting the mirror and reflecting into my eyes, dazzling. I blinked, seemed to be peering down an avenue of beacons. I cursed the idiot. The car was only ten yards behind, staying there. I slowed but it made no attempt to pass.

Jesus wept!

I thumped the wheel. An empty road. Just me and this idiot. Then my blood froze.

Was this how it had been for Eddie Morgan

last Friday night? Dazzling headlights in the mirror. The gradual murmurings of panic.

The road was wide, still empty. My foot went down. Sixty, seventy, eighty. My ageing Capri was reaching its zenith and could give little more. It bounced and shuddered on every pot hole. My foot ground the accelerator to the floor. The car behind hadn't lost an inch.

And still the lights!

I was gradually being blinded. The steering wheel had begun to slip in my moist palms. I missed a bend in the road and the tyres howled. And still the bastard hadn't budged! Still the lights!

I eased back my foot. The speedometer needle slowly slid back to forty. My clothes were pasted to my body, sweat irritated my eyes. And always those bloody lights blinding me!

Then suddenly, sweet bliss. The lights were gone. I was plunged into darkness. It took seconds for my addled brain to realise what was happening. The car swept by, cut in.

This was how Eddie Morgan died. But I wasn't drunk. I was stony cold sober, and scared. I swung the car in the opposite direction to that which they expected. There was the screech of tearing metal, tyres screaming. They spun. I didn't. I was past, my foot going down hard.

A short respite. They were soon back on my tail. Again the lights. Again I squinted. Same manoeuvre? Possibly. The road had narrowed. Humps and hollows. Houses. I remembered the old couple. How Morgan had fallen on the car horn, and the result.

I swallowed, said my little prayer. I'd be good in future, if only—

I hit the brakes hard, saw the curved drive loom, then spun the car at it. Gravel spit into the air. I scraped the privet hedge. The car shuddered to a stop in front of a large house. The other car hadn't followed me in. I saw it stop fifty yards down the road and begin to reverse. I could make out that it was a Rover, but not the registration number. There were two figures inside.

That's when I hit the horn and jammed my foot on the accelerator. The noise boomed through the night. The door of the house opened and a man stood framed against the light. He didn't concern me. I grinned as the Rover pulled away, watching till it vanished. A fist thumped on the roof and I decided it was time to move. I didn't need aggro from an irate householder. Quickly, I reversed out.

I took the scenic route home, a patchwork of narrow lanes and roads.

I had much to ponder on.

It was no consolation to be proved right. The itch between my shoulder blades had been real. I had been followed, probably from the day I came on the case. And the Rover was the same that had tagged me from the Spencer house earlier. But they had broken off the moment they realised I had spotted them. So how had they picked me up again? It was obvious. I had spoken to Irene Downes—so they guessed where I was heading. And why had they only now chosen to take me out of the game? Because I had got on to Eddie Morgan?

And who were Curly and Mute?

Who did they work for?

I reached town. My bones ached. My eyelids drooped. My empty stomach was a gnawing pain that demanded to be fed. But I still had one call to make.

* * *

I thumbed the bell for a good five minutes before the door opened. I pushed inside.

'We talk, Irene,' I hissed. 'We talk of Eddie Morgan, and Karen, and drugs.'

'Do we!' Her laugh was a snort of contempt.

'Eddie is dead!' I let the words explode. 'His brother didn't take the trouble to inform you. He doubted if you cared for each other. He presumed you were simply his current bit of stuff.'

I was thunderstruck by her reaction. She crumbled and the tears flowed. I recognised that she had actually loved him. I felt like a bastard, and it took the steam out of me. I found myself in the unlikely role of comforter.

But when she regained her composure the shock had loosened her tongue. There was a lot of talk before she got around to the point.

'Eddie wasn't a pusher,' she assured me. 'But he took a macabre pride in the fact that he could fix a purchaser with anything he required. He wasn't on drugs himself.'

I asked her to explain his relationship with Karen.

'Oh, that.' She toyed distractedly with the gold chain around her neck. 'There was no relationship, not really. She screwed up her face if a man even looked at her. But for a while she fascinated Eddie. So reserved, so prim and delicate. He wanted to get under her skin, see what made her tick. The same way he'd strip down a car engine if it wasn't running right.'

I asked if she was claiming that Eddie didn't introduce Karen to drugs.

'No, he did that all right.' She pointed to the window.

'On a clear day you can see right over the town to the hills beyond. Eddie invited her to come around if she wanted to do some sketching, that I'd be here to protect her honour. So she did. She was unlucky. Eddie was in one of his particularly playful moods. He slipped something into a drink and gave it to her. The girl flipped. She talked, hell how she talked.'

Interested, I asked, 'What did she talk

about?'

'The puppy she used to own, her dolls.' Irene's voice was very soft, almost a whisper. Her face remained stained with tears. 'Funny though, she never seemed to get past the age of sixteen, as if her life had stopped then. Eddie introduced her to other drugs, eventually heroin. She was a willing pupil. He liked to watch her, made her yap and bark like a dog. He called her his puppy bitch.'

Eddie Morgan had to have been sick in the head. And the same applied to Irene Downes. Bile rose in my throat. I strained to keep my voice flat.

'What were you doing while Eddie played his little games?'

'Don't get sanctimonious with me!' Her eyes blazed a second, then cooled. 'There was nothing I could do. I pleaded with him to leave her alone. She was harmless, sometimes even sweet. She had the idea that drugs made her like other people. She had a massive inferiority complex, and no amount of reassurance made her see it any other way.'

The anger hadn't left me. 'Why didn't you pack your bags and walk out on him?'

'I loved him!' she yelled. 'I couldn't leave him! There was a lot that was good in Eddie.'

It must have been buried deep! But what was the point! I'd never understand the female mind.

'And he grew bored with Karen,' I said

76

flatly.

'More or less,' Irene replied. 'Karen was a junkie by then, sticking needles into herself like a veteran. She needed more and more. And Eddie decided he could no longer help finance her habit. If she couldn't pay—hard luck. She cried, kept coming round here to plead. He told her to get on the streets and earn some money.'

I had already guessed what had become of Karen's possessions; the TV, the record player; now it was confirmed. She sold them to buy drugs, and finally there was nothing left to sell.

'Who did Eddie get the drugs from?' I asked, hoping that this might be the connection I was looking for, the explanation of why Morgan had suddenly bolted.

'I have no idea, and that is the truth. He only collected the drugs for Karen, excepting the grass and acid, which was for our own personal use.'

I changed tack. 'Karen came around here last Thursday, didn't she?'

Irene nodded. 'Half-past eight. She stayed half an hour. Eddie had phoned earlier to say he wouldn't be back till late. I told Karen this, but it seemed to take the full half hour for it to sink in.'

I asked if Karen had been carrying a holdall. The question seemed to puzzle her. She shook her head. I asked if Karen had wanted money.

'Forty pounds,' she said. 'I had no forty

77

pounds or I might have given it to her.' I asked where Karen had made for when she left here. 'I have no idea.'

'So tell me about the two men who called here last Friday looking for Eddie, probably masquerading as policemen.'

'Yes.' No lies now. 'Only they were not policemen. I have a good nose on me. Living with Eddie you soon develop one. They wanted Eddie, and ran through the flat like they owned it. They also mentioned Karen.'

'Did you give them Karen's address?' I asked. She nodded. 'And you sent them to Bolton as you did me?'

'For my pains—yes.' She sucked in her breath. 'I was mad. Eddie wouldn't say why he was leaving. He even took the cash from my handbag. We argued violently. He struck me. The only time he ever did that. So I wanted those men to find him and hurt him, but no more.' Her eyes met mine. 'Did they kill him?'

I'd been wondering when she'd get around to asking how Morgan died. I owed her nothing. I felt little but contempt for her. But I gave her the answer she wanted to hear.

'No. He died in a traffic accident. He was drunk and his car skidded into a tree.'

She sighed, conscience clearing. She thanked God. I asked what the two men had wanted with Eddie.

'I don't know—honestly. They weren't communicative.' She was starting to crumble again, eyes moistening. 'I presumed he'd pulled a stunt on them.'

'Such as?'

'Faulty equipment. A lot of stuff passed through his hands, some good, some bad. He also gambled. Sometimes he was flush with money and he'd spend it like water. Other times he'd be skint. He'd been stony broke for the past week. So perhaps he owed them money.'

'Or sold them bad heroin?' I offered drily.

'No!' Her eyes blazed again. 'He didn't deal in drugs. I swear to that.'

There were more questions I should have asked, but my mind had dulled. And no street walking for me tonight. Mrs Harker's, a meal, and a warm bed. It sounded like paradise.

CHAPTER NINE

Thursday; a jewel of a morning. No rain, and the mist clung only lightly to the ground; bitterly cold though. A short drive and I was back at the Georgian terrace.

For a change I had the Spencers together, though I spoke mainly to Val. Ian seemed more interested in the morning paper.

'So you knew Karen was an addict?' I was saying.

'I knew.' There was a depth of sadness in

her eyes that I wouldn't have thought this woman capable of. 'I became suspicious some weeks ago. Her health, the missing TV. I asked, but she refused to confirm or deny. Three days before she left I searched her room. I found a hypodermic needle. And so I confronted her. She screamed, and at one point seemed ready to attack me.'

'What did you do?'

'I gave her one week to pull herself together. If she hadn't, I threatened to take her to a doctor if I had to strap her into a wheelchair and push her there myself. I had already begun to make enquiries on how best to deal with the situation. At one time I thought the threat might be the reason she left.'

'But when she told you she was leaving you didn't try to dissuade her?'

'No.' Just a touch of testiness entered her voice. 'The phone rang, as I have already explained. And really, I didn't take her words seriously.'

'Why?' I asked.

'Mr Conroy—Karen was no angel. She was often sulky and bad tempered. She believed I was neglecting her, and her answer was to punish me by silence. So I let her. I decided it was time Karen stood on her own two feet. Her parents had cosseted her, and for the first year here I did the same. I loved the girl, but enough was enough. I had a life of my own, and she was old enough to understand that. So to punish me she ceased to confide in me. When she said she was leaving I thought it was just another ploy to make me feel sorry for her.'

I was beginning to learn a little more of Karen. I dropped the drugs angle.

'The men who came looking for her the next day—why didn't you mention them to the Richardsons when they visited you last Sunday?'

'Oh, that.' Val leaned back, whitened her bottom lip with her teeth. 'At first I took them to be policemen. They acted how policemen are supposed to act. I presumed Mrs Richardson had rung the local police station to report Karen missing. It only struck me as odd when they asked for the address of Karen's parents. Then it seemed unlikely that two plain-clothed policemen would enquire after Karen on the strength of a phone call from a woman who had experienced a vivid nightmare. A constable possibly, but not two detectives. It was then that I asked to see their warrant cards.

'The dark haired one smiled. "Oh, we're not policemen, love. Whatever gave you that idea? No, she has something that belongs to us." Then they left.'

I digested her words, then said, 'You haven't answered my question, Val.'

'Oh?' Bewildered, she stared at me. 'Karen

was looking for money the day before. She asked me, just to be awkward I suppose, giving me the obvious lie that she needed the money to buy a new coat. She got no money from me. I presumed she had borrowed some, and that was the reason they wanted her, and that was why she left. And I simply did not want to add more misery to the Richardsons. I did not want them to discover that Karen was an addict. Mr Richardson is already a sick man as you probably noticed.' I hadn't. 'This could push him over the edge. I hoped Karen would return before they had to know.'

'And you didn't tie these men into the nightmare?'

'The men came here a good twelve hours after the so-called vision,' she said drily. 'And Karen was long gone. And nightmare is what it was, as you very well know. Karen will show up, Mr Conroy, and I shall give her the money to settle her debts with those men, but no more. She is with a friend whose identity we simply don't know.'

Up until now everybody had been telling me Karen had no friends. I let it pass. I asked why she hadn't mentioned the two men to me when I spoke to her before.

'You were hired by the Richardsons, you would report back to them.' She paused. 'Do the Richardsons know about the drugs?'

'Not from me.'

'Keep it that way if you can. When you find

Karen, let me know first. I will see to her.'

A thought struck me. 'The holdall—Karen was seen later that night. There was no holdall.'

'Then she must have returned later that night to pack. I didn't see or hear her.'

That seemed to be that. Ian Spencer broke away from his newspaper long enough to see me out.

*   *   *

No strange men watching the office, nor had I been followed. I'd made sure of that. Mrs Harker passed on a message from Major Seddon. Nobody remotely resembling Karen had been in touch with the Samaritans, nor had the Salvation Army any knowledge of her.

In my office I picked up the phone and dialled. Mrs Richardson answered. I had no news, no good news that is, only a question. I described Curly and Mute.

'They didn't come to see you?' I asked.

Her voice was perplexed. 'No. No one has been.'

I trod carefully. 'Have any of your neighbours mentioned these men?'

'No—why—?' Her voice trailed off.

I tried to come up with a plausible line. 'A routine lead. I think these men may have been friends of Karen's. They were looking for her over the weekend. Do me a favour—ask your neighbours if they have seen these men—spoken to them. I don't think there is anything sinister in this, but I'd like to trace them. Who knows, they might have found her and our troubles will be over.'

If I could have bitten off my tongue I'd have chewed it up and swallowed it. I hoped to hell they hadn't found Karen, and I hoped I hadn't alarmed Mrs Richardson too much. But then, she was already convinced that her daughter was dead. A few meaningless platitudes and I hung up. Then out into the cold again.

*   *   *

Almost noon, and her eyes were still filled with sleep. She languidly moved aside and allowed me into the house.

She was tall and willowy, brown hair rolling down to her waist; a little too thin, but her small unslung breasts roamed sweetly inside her jumper. She was Sally Benson, daughter of the man who owned the sweet stall in the arcade. The girl someone had informed me had encountered Karen last Thursday night.

'That's right.' She sniffled a little as she sat on a stool by the kitchen table. 'A van. A big one. Dark. Karen sat in the front. I was on my way to a party with a bloke I'd met, sometime before eleven. We were crossing the car-park in Wendover Street when this van roared away. I scraped my knee and dropped the bottle of

84

wine I was holding. I was mad as hell.'

She wandered off tack for a while, then came back to the point.

'I glimpsed four faces. The driver was a bloke. I've an idea I've seen him before but don't ask me where—I don't remember. I think the others were all women, though it was dark and I'm not quite sure. I recognised Karen because she was closest to me, against the window. I remember thinking she looked like a little white ghost. So sad and lost. Next day I went to the arcade to find out from Karen who was driving the van. But she wasn't there.'

I wanted background information. I asked if she had first met Karen at the arcade.

'No,' she said. 'Methusalah's Pit.'

The widening of my eyes made her chuckle. She had perked up, grinning.

'Wouldn't expect to find shy little Karen there. Mind, she worked as a waitress, strictly legit. It wasn't compulsory to take a ride with a customer, despite the rumours you hear. But Karen was braver than me. She lasted a fortnight. I only made it through four hectic nights. A bit less than a year ago it would be. We got along like a house on fire.' Another raised eyebrow brought another chuckle. 'Okay. But you see, I'm a talker, and nobody could accuse Karen of being likewise. We were the ideal match.

'She was a gutsy little thing in her own way.

I think she was fighting her shyness, and you can't afford to be shy at the Pit. But obviously her experiment failed. I suggested the arcade if she fancied a little casual work. In fact, I introduced her around.'

'Did she ever mention a man named Eddie Morgan?'

'No. But I've not seen much of Karen lately.'

I recounted some of Karen's history; the rape, the abortion. I studied her face as it fell through a multitude of sad emotions.

She commented that it explained a great deal. I agreed. And I had an idea I was about to fracture our budding relationship.

'Just how close were your father and Karen?'

'Not that close.' She startled me by throwing her head back and laughing. 'Where did you pluck that old chestnut from?'

'The way your father reacted when I mentioned Karen,' I explained. 'Something one of the other stallholders hinted.'

'It's a sick joke,' she said. 'They were friends—nothing more. To Dad she was the daughter he always longed for. Oh, no need to look at me that way. I'm his natural born all right. But I'm like Mum in his eyes, flighty and man mad. She ran off some twelve years back. Karen was his idea of what a young lady should be. I welcomed their friendship. It took a lot of pressure off me.

'He even took her to the Lakes.' I recalled the sketches of Windermere, Val Spencer mentioning the times Karen spent away from home. 'Then the relationship soured. They didn't fall out, nothing so simple. You see, word leaked out that they had been away together, and the tongues began to wag. Much gossip and sniggering. Dad couldn't take that. He practically cut Karen stone dead from then on.'

She showed me to the door, wishing me good luck in my search for Karen.

*　　　*　　　*

'I can shout even louder,' I threatened.

George Benson glanced over my shoulder at the curious faces that turned our way. He backed down grimly, called for someone to watch his stall. We moved to a quiet café at the top of the arcade.

'All right,' he said. 'So we were friends, but no more. I took her to the Lakes. I liked her company. I liked to watch her sketching.'

'Plurely platonic,' I commented drily. 'Holding hands in the park?'

'Not true!' Then he wavered. 'We walked through the park once or twice. Perhaps we did touch hands. Perhaps she said something to amuse me.'

'Why did you cut her from your life, George?'

87

'I explained. People were sniggering behind my back. I might not rate very high in your eyes, but I have my pride, my self-respect.' His voice had slipped to a low growl. 'They were insinuating that I was having an affair with a girl younger than my own daughter. And it was untrue!'

I wasn't buying his story. He might be a pompous and introverted individual, but he was surely capable of taking a few sniggers on the chin. And if he had been as fond of Karen as he claimed, he simply wouldn't have cut her off that way, he wouldn't have hurt her. There had to be more, but I couldn't budge him. I switched direction.

'Did you know Karen was a drug addict?'

'Hell no!' The shock that registered on his face seemed genuine enough. 'I haven't spoken to her in weeks. The Thursday when she hovered near my stall was the closest she came to opening her mouth.'

There was little more to be got from George Benson, for the time being that is.

I killed a long afternoon on the snooker table with a few mates. I won a couple of quid. It did something to cheer me up.

*　　　*　　　*

Methusalah's Pit was the sort of hole where you took a mate to guard your back when you wanted a leak. It resembled a cave; garish serpents and imps crawled the walls and ceiling, dark corners where everything went and very often did. It wasn't the sort of place a man took his wife on their anniversary, or any other occasion. The Pit owed its existence to the most casual and fleeting encounters of the flesh.

Very noisy tonight, despite the early hour. I found a table as far away from the stage as possible. An emaciated comic was going through his spiel. Nobody seemed to be laughing, or even listening. I drank some, idled, then in a moment of calm got the waitress to sit, simply by the crinkling of a five-pound note in my fingers. Bleached blonde, much creamy breast and mascara on view, plenty of wet lip and tongue. She reminded me of a little white rabbit. I asked if she remembered Karen Richardson. It took much time and concentration.

'Oh, yeah. Quiet little piece. Ages ago since she worked here. Couldn't stand the pace I expect.' Bleak and weary eyes took in the room. 'And who can blame her?'

I had already decided I was wasting my time when the little darling had me sitting up.

'She was in here last week,' she said. 'Thursday night I think.'

'What time?' I asked.

'Not sure.' Flick of a thoughtful tongue. The fiver was slipping away and she knew it. 'I think she spoke to Maureen. Hang on.' She was gone, but soon back with a rush. 'That's right. Last Thursday. She was looking for Jimmy Keegan.'

A new name to me. I asked just who the hell was Jimmy Keegan. She shrugged.

'Nobody knows. Sort of acts like he owns the place, like he's management—only he isn't. We think he's related to the owner but we don't know. He comes in here a lot.'

'Is he in tonight?' I asked eagerly.

'No. Haven't seem him in a week—which is a long time for him to stay away.'

'Did Karen find Keegan?' I asked.

'No. He wasn't here.'

More bad news. I asked if Karen had said why she wanted Keegan.

The girl almost met my eyes for the first time, but not quite. Probably a trick of the light. She made a plunging motion into her forearm.

'Probably that. Maureen guessed so anyway. And nobody knows more about that sort of thing than Maureen.'

'Keegan's a pusher?' I asked.

The girl was ready to flee. Her voice rose. 'How should I know! Lots of people use drugs in this place. It helps them forget. Best to say nothing. And I've said nothing to you, have I?'

'Not a bloody thing,' I agreed. I showed her the sketch of Eddie Morgan.

'Never seen him, but all men look alike to me.'

She snatched the fiver and was on her feet. Then she hesitated. She bent close to my ear, and her breath was surprisingly pleasant.

'God didn't bless me with much of a face but I'm happy with it. And Maureen told Karen to look for Keegan at Raven's. He spends a lot of time there. A disco, near the town centre. There is a rumour that it has the same owner as this place.'

She was gone, and more than a little bit scared. I'd have liked a word with the mysterious Maureen, but decided that might have drawn a little too much attention to me. Anyway, I had another call to make. And I was getting closer to Karen. The car-park where Sally Benson had spotted Karen in the van was across the road from Raven's. I was fast plugging the gaps in Karen's movements last Thursday.

*   *   *

More of a club than a disco; the age groupings varied; a plush restaurant; three separate dance floors. I made it to the one in the cellar where the younger crowd gathered; average age I guessed to be early twenties.

The music roared bewilderingly loud, smashed my ear-drums, made me wince at each decibel. The lights that flashed above and around hurt my eyes. Not my sort of place, my idea of paradise. All tits and bums encased in tight denim and silk, the air stiff with the electricity of as yet unrequited sexual couplings. The heady aroma of perfume made me a little nauseous.

I began to ask questions; and the conversation with the second barman I approached proved fruitful.

'I saw her,' he said. 'Thursday last. Nice looking kid in a gaunt sort of way. She stumbled about the place, seemed to be looking for somebody.'

I asked if he had spoken to her.

'No. She never made it this far.' He pointed to nowhere in particular. 'Settled down over there. I saw her talking to Sharon Walsh.' I cocked an eyebrow in question. 'I used to go to school with Sharon. No beauty, and a little short on charm, but willing, and game for anything. And no, she's not here tonight. She lives in the Hutch.'

The mention of the Hutch sent a tremor down my spine. He left for a short time to serve somebody.

'Odd though, they left together,' the barman continued on his return. 'Her, Sharon, another girl, and a bloke named Keegan.'

Keegan again. So Karen had found him. I asked if Keegan was in tonight.

'Not your night, is it mate?' He laughed. 'No, I haven't seen Keegan since that night.'

'Who is he?'

'Blowed if I know. Mr Big—ponces in here

like he's taken over from God. That's all I know about him.'

More questions. He began to explain what had happened that night. He pointed to the main doors.

'Must have been after ten. Keegan appears and swaggers across the room. The tall piece with the red hair and cheeky arse.'

Another pointed finger. Two girls dancing on a raised dais; eyes glazed, looking nowhere, gyrating. The redhead wore a short yellow dress, perspiration glistened on a lovely face.

'He spoke to her,' the barman went on. 'Just for a second or two. He helped her down and they disappeared into the back. She's wearing a coat when they emerge. Anyway, they stop at the table where Sharon and the girl you're looking for are sitting. And the outcome is— all four left together.'

Across the street to the car-park, where they almost knocked down Sally Benson. I was still making progress. I tipped the barman a quid. He was a gem.

I wasted a little more time, then positioned myself by the door marked PRIVATE. She leapt off the dais and was almost past me before I could grab her arm. She swung around, palm flat and ready to swing. The green eyes cut a path through my skull.

'You can't afford the price, friend!'

What price? I hadn't made an offer, and I certainly wasn't paying for what she had on her

93

mind. I tried a smile, held up my palms in reconciliation. It didn't work. Her eyes still blistered my skin.

'Excuse the hands,' I said. 'But all I want is a little chat.'

'Got a talking one have you! How novel!'

Talking what for God's sake! Maybe the drink and the musky odour of her sweat was getting to me.

'Jimmy Keegan,' I said quickly. 'A friend of yours I believe? I'm looking for him. We used to be mates.'

A curious light touched her eyes, the flush on her cheeks lessened, but her voice remained sharp and dismissive.

'Sorry, friend, never heard of him. What's your name? If I ever run across this Keegan bloke I'll let him know you were asking.'

Dumb insolence, or contempt. It could have been either or a mixture of both. I didn't dwell on it. Her proximity was disconcerting, and she knew it. She stepped closer and we were almost touching.

'The name is Conroy,' I muttered. 'How about Karen Richardson—heard of her?'

No response. There was a smile at the back of her eyes now. And despite the noise in the place I could almost hear the wheels in her brain ticking over. I repeated what the barman had told me. She bit her lip thoughtfully, then shrugged lightly.

'Hang around,' she said. 'I'll be back.'

She was, two minutes later. Her coat was open and I glimpsed the yellow dress. She hadn't bothered to change. Her voice was filled with promise and mischief.

'We'll go somewhere quiet—and talk.'

The barman winked in my direction as I left with the redhead on my arm.

CHAPTER TEN

I dug my fingers into the flesh of her buttocks to raise her higher; rolling palms over smooth hills and hollows that were now slick with sweat; fingers finding moist and secret crevices. She moaned deep in her throat at my touch. My world was veiled in fiery red as I viewed it through strands of sweet smelling hair. Her wet tongue and lips began to work again. On my mouth, my neck. They were tongue and lips that knew everything, had no secrets; mechanical like much of her love-making, finding nerve endings instantly, without that delightful voyage of exploration.

But she was good. Christ! How good she was! A few more seconds and I'd be ready again. I vaguely wondered what passed through her mind as she worked so solemnly. I didn't reflect on it too long.

Her name was Anne Lindsay. Her profession—dancer.

The somewhere quiet she brought me was her flat. And it was quite a pad. An apartment block at the moneyed end of town, the fittings plush and rich, filled with expensive gadgetry, carpets that reached the ankles. I wondered how much a dancer earned, and guessed it wouldn't pay a week's rent on this place. Something I found very interesting.

We talked, just a little. She recounted her version of what happened in Raven's the previous Thursday night.

During a rest period Jimmy Keegan entered. They spoke, and she mentioned a headache. He went off to ask the manager if it was okay for her to leave. She resumed her dance on the dais. Jimmy was soon back, saying he'd fixed it for her to leave. He offered to run her home. She accepted.

Leaving, Jimmy spotted two girls he knew. He stopped to say hello. It was true that all four left the club together, but pure coincidence. They parted on the pavement. The two girls were moving on to another disco. Keegan drove Anne home. He dropped her on the street outside. He did not come inside, she informed me with a smile.

One of the girls did fit the description of Karen, but she couldn't swear to it. She had a blinding headache and was impatient to return home.

She was vague on the subject of Keegan. She had met him several times at the club. He had tried to date her, but he wasn't her type; too brash and aggressive. She didn't know how he earned a living, or where he lived. As far as she knew he was not connected with the owner of Raven's, whoever that might be.

Her story was reasonable, if you discounted some puzzling points. Why had she denied knowing Keegan when I first approached her? And she certainly hadn't needed the manager's permission to leave the club with me. So why on that particular night had she needed Keegan to act as go-between? And Sally Benson had positively stated that there were four people in the van as it pulled off the car-park, and one of these she identified as Karen.

And what occurred next was even more puzzling.

Now I'm not ugly, but then, I'm not exactly handsome; two broken noses and an assortment of kicks and punches about the face had seen to that. Beautiful women just didn't go weak at the knees when I moved in on them. But suddenly, that seemed to be the effect I was having on Anne Lindsay. Ten minutes after we entered the flat we were in bed. And she was pumping me for information about Karen Richardson, whispered questions as she nibbled my ear, stroking with warm palms. I gave out snippets of information to keep her sweet, small hints that I knew more than I did. And if this was her own particular

97

interrogation technique, I was all in favour of prolonging it.

Her tongue and lips moved down again, made tiny sucking noises as they progressed. My hand slid round to take a breast and manipulate the hardened tip. She moaned on cue.

A noise? Outside? The hairs on my neck prickled. I asked if she had heard it.

'No,' she mumbled. Whatever had disturbed me was soon forgotten as her knees clamped tight around me. 'Good boy. Good boy.'

I was trying. Oh hell, I was.

That's when the door sprang open. The sudden light dazzled me. I covered my eyes and squinted through splayed fingers. The blanket was torn aside, and a heavy palm slapped against Anne's bare skin.

'Up you get, sweetheart.' The voice was quiet and filled with cold humour. 'I hope you gave him something memorable to take with him.'

Anne was climbing off me, breasts still thrusting and streaked with red finger marks. There was just a hint of malice as she stood at the side of the bed and glanced down at me. And she wasn't shy, all glistening nudity in front of three men. I don't think she even noticed.

And the two men?

Curly and Mute of course. They had found me—not the other way round. Curly stood at

98

the side of the bed, Mute on guard by the door. Their grins were open and mocking.

'Learn anything?' Curlcy asked Anne.

'Not a lot. He's a comic. Hired by the girl's parents. He doesn't know much. Probably not bright enough to catch a cold in Iceland.' She continued to study me. She knew that given a chance I'd strangle her, that and my naked helplessness seemed to amuse her. She quipped drily, 'Don't get blood on the carpet.'

She strolled casually from the room. I heard the rattle of pans in a distant kitchen. I was erased from her mind; little more than a piece of useless meat that had amused her for a while.

'You going to lie there all night, tosser?' Curly was asking, but definitely not requesting.

I realised I hadn't spoken since these men had burst in. I didn't feel scared, just numb. My skin was clammy as Anne's sweat dried on me, turning to ice.

'Move it, tosser.' A little menace had crept into Curly's voice. 'And don't even think about screaming.'

A knife had appeared in his hand and he traced it across my chest. He laughed harshly, said something about carving the Sunday joint.

And oh what a smart bastard I was. And how Anne Lindsay must have sniggered. I was a bloody fool! Two minutes to throw a coat over a dress? Two minutes to make a quick telephone call was more accurate. I'd been set up like a lamb for the slaughter.

'Come on, tosser!' Curly prodded me with the knife. Mute came a little closer. 'I'll use this. We're taking you for a ride.'

Oh, hell, nobody used lines like that these days. We were playing out a scene from a gangster movie. This was a bad dream. But dream or not, I was standing, shivering, reaching towards terror. These bastards meant to kill me!

'Am I allowed to dress?' The voice wasn't mine, surely, not that thin choked whine.

'Sure you are.' Curly laughed. 'Don't want the sight of that great pecker scaring old ladies, do we?'

So I dressed, and it took some time, seemingly hours to fasten my shoelaces. My hands shook. They escorted me to the door, one on either side.

Outside. A long carpeted corridor. I took a deep breath, pushing back the rising panic. I knew I had to do something before we left this building. Time wasn't on my side.

We had reached the stairs and I noticed the glass-encased fire alarm. Curly was leading, foot on the third step. Mute gripped my right arm as though he sensed something was about to happen. He was right. I was suddenly mad. They were thugs, little removed from animals.

I swung my left elbow like a piston. The glass cover shattered. I hit the plunger. The building erupted with a high pitched whine.

Startled, Curly swung, just in time for his nose to collide with my boot. He pitched backwards down the stairs. My twisting momentum sent Mute tumbling after him, but only for a few steps. He took the pose of a fighter as he looked up at me, legs spread, and there was the glint of steel in his right fist. Behind him, Curly was coming to his feet. There was no sign of his knife. The building had come to life. There was a scream somewhere above. Curly was the bright one. He caught Mute by the shoulder and pulled him back.

'Let's get out of here,' he yelled. 'We'll deal with this bastard some other time.'

Reluctantly, Mute conceded. They passed from sight around a bend in the stairs. I heard their receding feet. I didn't follow. The thought of a knife darting at my gut scared the hell out of me.

And doors were slamming everywhere, voices. Down the corridor I caught the glimpse of an old man in a dressing gown. No Anne. I pondered on whether to go back, skin the bitch alive. But now wasn't the time.

I raced down the stairs, checked to make sure Curly and Mute were not about, and took a roundabout route to the office. In the distance I heard the sound of a fire engine klaxon splitting the night.

*   *   *

101

Friday; another Friday; more rain lashing against the window. I shuddered at the urgent jangle.

I hate phones; especially in the morning, or late at night; doom-laden purveyors of misery.

It was Mrs Richardson, and I silently cursed. I'd forgotten her. Mrs Harker had left a note on the pad saying the woman had tried to contact me the preceding afternoon. I quickly apologised.

The conversation didn't take long. She possibly solved one problem, but created another.

'You were right,' she said. 'But not quite. Somebody was in the neighbourhood asking questions about Karen. But it was an elderly woman.' I nearly dropped the phone as it singed my palm. 'She questioned my next door neighbour.

'She claimed to be an old friend of the family, and couldn't recall having seen Karen lately. She made a specific point of asking my neighbour if she had seen Karen last weekend. My neighbour obviously gave a negative reply. From her description I'm positive I don't know the woman.'

Mrs Richardson passed on the description to me. A little more chat to cool her nerves and I hung up.

I was soon dialling. I spoke quickly to cut out any possible interruptions. I had a pal on the local newspaper, Malcolm Fairhurst, and he was a mine of information. He promised to ring back.

Mrs Harker appeared. We shared a coffee, then she retreated to her outer sanctum and her knitting.

I massaged my knee as the odd twinge began to crawl up my leg. I leaned back, lit a cigarette, and pondered on my conversation with Mrs Richardson.

So who was the elderly woman who had taken the trouble to travel to Birmingham to enquire after Karen?

I had no answer, only the gut feeling that she was connected with Curly and Mute. And I'd been careful yesterday. I was sure Curly and Mute hadn't followed me. If they had, I'd have spotted them. But they'd got to me eventually, thanks to that redheaded bitch Anne Lindsay. Twice now they'd come close to picking me up, twice I'd slipped through their fingers. I shuddered. I probably wouldn't be so lucky a third time.

So why were Eddie Morgan and Karen so important to these people? Had they already found Karen—and dealt with her as they had Morgan?

Drugs?

Karen was an addict—certainly.

Morgan had a contact who supplied him with drugs.

It was possible, but I didn't think it likely. Then again, why not? Had Karen stumbled into something that night—something big? Something that perhaps involved the movement of drugs? Had she involved Morgan?

I recalled the owner of the garage where Morgan worked. Morgan had started last Friday in good humour. He makes a phone call, cries off work to visit the dentist, and returns some time later in an agitated state. He flees town. Later that night he is dead.

I glanced at my watch. Time to get back to work. I grabbed my coat and was quickly on the street.

Cars lined the kerb as usual. I barely spared them a glance. I reached my Capri that was parked on a scrap of waste ground I had made my own. I cursed as I noticed the busted wing. Something else to hold against Curly and Mute. Then suddenly, as I turned the key in the lock, my hair stood on end.

I jerked around.

It must have been my talk with Mrs Richardson that had alerted some frozen cell in my brain. I had just glimpsed a face behind the wheel of a battered Mini. It was a face I had seen before, twice. Once peeping around a door in the Forger, and once encountered on a dark street in the dead of night. The face had worn different ages, appeared under different hats, but I was sure it was the same, and fifty yards along the street I was seeing it again.

I broke into a run.

Too late!

She had spotted my intention. The Mini bolted from the kerb. A horn blared, tyres screeched. The Mini vanished around a corner before I even had the chance to catch the mud splattered number plate. I cursed, thumped my fist in frustration.

I'd blown it! A little thought, a little patience, and I could have had her!

I walked slowly back to my car. Belatedly, my brain cells began to function. I had been under surveillance from two teams. Curly and Mute, and the old lady. Had she trailed me yesterday? I didn't think so. I'd been too careful. So why was she back today? I had no answer.

I drove in circles for some minutes.

Nothing followed.

CHAPTER ELEVEN

The Hutch!

No poet in the darkest depths of torment could do justice to the Hutch.

Dark and grim, grey and bleak, occasional splashes of peeling yellow around the windows, concrete and glass. I trembled the length of my spine.

I'd moved here with my wife after I'd left the police force. I was at the Motor Works, most of my money going on booze, tumbling quickly down the road to alcoholism and not giving a damn how quickly I got there.

I hated the Hutch. The lift that never worked, the stink of dog shit in the stair wells, the wind that howled around the place and almost drove me crazy, the thin walls that carried every secret from one flat to the next, the whimpering in the night when it seemed the Hutch itself was weeping.

My wife stuck it for six months, then cleared out. I didn't blame her. I even sympathised. But a barrier of hate was growing between us, one that could never be torn down. And I would always remember her parting words. 'Your leg! That is your excuse for everything. Does your leg make you drink! You only limp when you are feeling sorry for yourself!'

The door slammed and she was gone from my life. But her words helped, for they came close to the truth, and would always remind me of what I was becoming. A drunk. A cynic. A maudlin fool. Next day I moved out of the Hutch and back to Mrs Harker's.

And here I was again, treading familiar balconies, the howling wind whipping around my head. I soon found Sharon Walsh, the girl who sat at the same table as Karen in Raven's.

Early twenties, small but perky breasts, quite pretty but for a somewhat mean mouth. I tried hard not to dislike her at first sight.

One of the traumas of my life had been

when I discovered that mean people really did exist away from the television screen, and they didn't always wear black hats.

You see, I'm a natural born bastard; what in these modern times would be rather chic and termed a love child. In those days it was different. Mothers warned their kids to stay away from me. I was tainted. But that was way in the past. And far from embittering me, discounting my darkest moments, it had left me with a deep compassion for the misfits of this world, amongst whose number I included myself.

Now I studied the mean mouth of Sharon Walsh and tried not to be influenced by it.

She showed me into the living room where the furniture was cheap and tatty, but spotlessly clean. I was soon painfully aware of the wind that rattled the windows. I heard a television in the adjoining flat, the flush of a distant toilet. She sat, and smoothed her skirt. She was happy to talk.

'I never met Karen before that night,' she said. 'I noticed her moving through the tables, looking for somebody. She seemed very nervous. Finally, she sat, next to me. I knew her problem without asking. I had once almost travelled the same road.'

'Who was she looking for?' I asked, though I already knew the answer.

'Jimmy Keegan,' Sharon replied.

I asked for a description, and she gave me

107

one.

'Keegan is a pusher?' I asked.

'Jimmy is a bit of everything.' She leaned forward with her elbows on her knees. 'A Mr Fix-it. Whether he is a pusher as such, I wouldn't know. Though he probably knows where to lay his hands on the stuff. But he talks big, which tends to make me think he isn't very important in himself. I'd met him a couple of times before that night. So when Karen reached my table and asked if I knew Jimmy, I told her to sit. He might turn up, he might not, no point fretting.

'She just sat there, eyes flying all over the place. Half an hour later Jimmy slouched in. He went to speak to one of the dancers. Karen was ready to get up and approach him. I told her to wait. Never press.

'Anyway, after the dancer, Anne Lindsay her name turned out to be, had collected her coat, they headed our way. I made sure Jimmy saw us and stopped. He asked if I'd like to go to a party. I jumped at the chance. Jimmy took me to a party once before. Real men, plenty of good food and drink.'

I listened intently, my ears pricked at every word. At last I was getting somewhere. Her voice rolled on.

'That's when he noticed Karen. I don't think he recognised her immediately. When he did he smiled. Sure, she could come to the party also, no problem, and he'd sort things out for her. And okay, so she was skint, he'd think of an amenable form of payment. So the four of us left.

'We took the north route out of town. Ten minutes later we were in Westholme. The house was a massive stone affair at the end of a long driveway. It was all lit up, great spanking new cars outside, even a Rolls. We parked a little way back, under the trees. Jimmy sent me and Anne inside where a man greeted us. He said it was good to see me again. I was pleased he remembered.'

'What happened to Keegan?' I asked.

She fixed me with a sharp glance that said I was an idiot. 'That's why he parked under the trees. He was making it with Karen. He's freaky that way. He likes to do it in the back of his van. He has it fitted out special.'

I was beginning to feel sick again. I asked for the identity of the man who greeted her at the door.

'Jack Evans. A big guy in his fifties with a balding head, often gets his photo in the papers.'

I knew the man. My heart began to thump madly. It was all I could do to hold back on a low whistle. I asked her about the party.

'A real turn on.' Sharon licked her lips. 'Everybody drunk, but merry with it, couples slipping off into dark corners.' She giggled. 'There were no wives of course.'

Of course. 'And Karen?'

That puzzled her. 'I never saw her after I left the van. Jimmy had come inside, I know that. I guess she was around somewhere, but I wasn't giving much thought to Karen. I stuck close to Jack Evans. He was the one with the real money.'

I was growing quite fond of Sharon. I thought maybe the lip had fooled me.

'Anne Lindsay had drifted off and I had manoeuvred myself onto Jack's knee,' she went on. 'Then this bloke interrupts. A phone call for Jack in the den, urgent. He cursed, and went to answer it. A few minutes later he was back, and not very happy. He shouted Keegan over and they talked in whispers. Then I saw them slip out. I was curious, so I peeked through the window. They got into Keegan's van and drove off.'

'What time was this?' I asked.

'Must have been around midnight.'

'How long were they gone?'

'A couple of hours before I saw them again,' Sharon said. 'Too long for me. I'd blown my chance with Jack. I ended up with a jockey. Jack didn't look too happy, nor did Keegan, who was having a fit of the sulks. Anyway, I was reaching the pink elephant stage. Next I knew it was morning and the jockey was snoring in my ear.'

'And you still hadn't seen Karen?'

'No. Perhaps she had gone off with one of the blokes,' she offered. 'Perhaps Jimmy had fixed her up and she'd wandered home.'

I asked about the relationship between Keegan and Evans.

'Friendly.' She frowned in concentration. 'I think Keegan works for Jack.' I asked if she knew where Keegan lived. She shook her head. 'Jack will probably know.'

No doubt he would, but I wasn't about to ask Jack Evans any questions—yet.

I thanked Sharon, and left.

*   *   *

He was caretaker, and general handyman at the apartment block where Anne Lindsay lived. He made sure the central heating worked, and was generally on hand to listen to the residents' complaints—which were multitude. He caught the flak while the owners swanned around the Continent. It didn't seem to have soured him. He enjoyed life and liked people, as a whole. He was in his sixties, a widower with seven grandchildren scattered around the world. A little wizened, but still the possessor of a sharp wit and keen eye.

We passed a pleasant afternoon in his tiny flat in the basement. I listened to his fund of stories and we played a few hands of poker. I seemed to have lightened a dull day. He accepted without question that I was working on a divorce case that involved one of his residents, Anne Lindsay.

I was in luck. The girl wasn't a favourite of his. She didn't smile or greet him when they passed. She failed to acknowledge his presence as a human being. In fact, she was a stuck-up cow.

Yes, he had often seen a man leaving her flat. His description fitted Jack Evans. But there was more. On a couple of occasions he had seen a younger man. Tall, in his twenties, good looking. I was disappointed that the description didn't fit Keegan, but happy to have the information.

I felt a traitor for what happened when the man was called upstairs. I took the chance to do a little thieving. There was a board outside his door, keys hanging on hooks beside the appropriate flat number. When a resident misplaced his key he rang for the caretaker who let him into the building, then his flat. I lifted the key to the main door and the one to Anne Lindsay's flat, then slipped away. I was gone less than half an hour. I gave him some cock and bull story about my car and a double yellow line. The keys were soon back on the rack. We whiled away more time.

*   *   *

Night had fallen.

No lights shone in the office, which shouldn't have surprised me as Mrs Harker invariably left around four. But after recent experiences my nerves were still very much on edge.

I climbed the stairs warily. I slipped the key in the lock and softly eased the door. Not a sound, not a whisper, only the hum of traffic on the street. I clicked on the light and blinked.

The sudden explosion of the telephone almost had me leaping through my skin. I cursed and took a deep breath. I moved to the inner office. The light slanted in from the street outside and threw my shadow onto the wall. I tossed the evening newspaper onto the desk. I picked up the receiver.

'I've bcen trying to get you all afternoon, Frankie. I've got the info you wanted.'

Malcolm Fairhurst, my pal on the local newspaper, had come through, as I knew he would. As usual, he croaked as if he'd been running for a bus—and missed it.

'So let's have it,' I demanded.

'Raven's and Methusalah's Pit have the same owner,' he answered. 'And wait for this, the registered owner is Doreen Evans.'

What the hell was that supposed to convey! I asked for the identity of Doreen Evans.

'Pillock! She is only the ex-wife of Jack Evans!'

I grinned in the darkness. I was indeed a pillock. I had asked Malcolm to check on the ownership because someone had mentioned that Jimmy Keegan might be related to that owner, for no stronger motive than that. Now it seemed that everything today had been coming up Jack Evans. Jack Evans, the local lad who made good, one of the famous sons of this town.

'And does that mean Jack is the real owner?' I asked.

'It means it is quite possible,' Malcolm replied. 'Jack was in trouble with the law some time back, and maybe he wasn't able to obtain a licence. The Pit's been open some eleven years and was maybe part of the divorce settlement. They split around that time. Jack went on to bigger and better things. Doreen spends a lot of time in Italy these days.'

A little more chat. Raven's had been open some six months. The manager had a good reputation.

'I'll be in touch, Mal,' I ended. 'I might want a chat about Jack Evans, so do some digging. I've an idea it might be worth your while.'

I clicked on the desk lamp and began to scrawl on a note pad. If I still hadn't solved the riddle of Karen's disappearance, I had at least plotted a good portion of her progress on the day she suddenly decided to leave town. Right up to eleven at night, give or take certain adjustments to the time scale.

9.00 am: Rises, moves about her flat, meets Val at the bottom of the stairs.

10.00 am: The arcade, listless, nervous.

11.00 am: Waits for Eddie Morgan at the

garage. He arrives, sends her away.
1.00 pm: The pub.
1.30 pm: The cinema.
2.00 pm: Wanders the park.
6.00 pm: The pub again.
7.00 pm: Back at her flat.
8.30 pm: Morgan's flat.
9.00 pm: Methusalah's Pit.
10.00 pm: Raven's.
11.00 pm: The party.

So I had accomplished what I set out to do on the day I began to look for Karen. But it hadn't brought me closer to finding her. The most important period still lay shrouded. What had happened to Karen after Jimmy Keegan left her in that van? That I still had to discover.

I pushed aside the pad. I knuckled my tired and gritty eyes. I lit a cigarette and the taste was sour and bitter in my lungs. I mashed it out.

The words seemed to leap out and blind me. Just a small piece in thick black ink in the late news column of the folded newspaper.

Terry Parkinson, 22, barman at a local nightspot, Raven's, was assaulted in broad daylight in the lane behind his home. The attack took place at lunch-time. His wallet and watch were stolen. His condition is not serious, but he is being detained in hospital for observation.

I threw my mind back to Raven's, fixing the

face of the barman I had spoken to. There was a name pinned to the lapel of his jacket. And that name was—Terry!

Oh, sweet Jesus! What had I done!

Another appalling thought struck me. If the young man had been beaten because he spoke to me, and I was accepting that as fact, the stolen watch and money meant nothing. And had he mentioned a certain name?

My hands trembled as I thumbed through the telephone directory. Walsh was listed many times, but none resided at the Hutch.

I was soon on the street, into my car. The tyres spun and skidded as I drove like the lunatic I probably was in those moments. I didn't glance in the mirror. I didn't give a damn if I was followed. I was soon at the Hutch, running up the stairs, hammering on Sharon Walsh's door.

It opened a crack, and a tentative face peered around. I sighed, but there was fear and hatred in her eyes.

'You bastard,' she hissed. 'They beat me up. They said they'd cut me. You didn't warn me what would happen if I spoke to you.'

I tried to explain. The inadequate words tripped off my tongue. I tried to ease my way inside, apologise, anything, just to soften the accusation in those eyes. But she wouldn't budge. Her voice grew more strident.

'Listen to me good, you bastard. I never saw Karen Richardson that night. I met Jimmy

116

Keegan and Anne Lindsay at Raven's. We went to a party at Jack Evans's place. Jack and Jimmy never left the house. I can vouch for that. I lied to you before. I am now giving you the truth. I have never met Karen Richardson. I have never heard of her.' She took a deep breath. 'Now get the hell away from here before somebody sees you.'

The door slammed in my face. Stunned, I stared at it a long time. I turned and leaned against the railings. The wind blew through me. I was chilled, and scared, and angry. I studied the town as it squatted in the valley beneath me. Lights everywhere, twinkling, a haze of smoke creeping upwards to the glowering sky, the ribbon of motorway curling into the distance.

They were down there someplace; Curly, Mute, the old woman, Jack Evans, Jimmy Keegan, and the answers to the mystery I had become embroiled in.

But where was Karen?

What had she stumbled into that was so important to these people? And Mrs Richardson's vision? A nightmare? That now seemed the most likely answer. They were still hunting Karen days later. So the inference was that Karen was still very much alive—unless. I shuddered.

Hell! There was little point in pursuing that line. I brushed a hand across my tired eyes.

I had brought pain and grief to two

117

innocents. I recalled talking to Anne Lindsay in Raven's, how I'd pointed to the barman and told her the boy had seen her and Keegan stop at the table where Karen sat with Sharon Walsh. They'd got to the boy. They'd beaten him. He'd repeated our conversation. The name Sharon Walsh had come out. Of course they might already have known where Sharon lived. But she only became important when it became clear that I knew she existed, or they'd have got to her much sooner.

So what was I left with to connect Karen with Keegan and Evans?

The word of Sally Benson, who glimpsed Karen in the van that night, on a dimly lit car-park. It wasn't much. And Sally had not been able to identify the other three occupants of the van, though she had an idea she knew the driver. From her time at the Pit? It was possible.

I walked the streets that night. I prayed that a dark car would slide to the kerb beside me. I wanted to fight—and hurt!

The keys that would gain me access to Anne Lindsay's flat burned holes in my pocket, freshly cut and shining, and waiting. But my mood was too black, too dangerous. I might beat the truth from her—but I might also kill her!

I encountered nothing.

CHAPTER TWELVE

A terrible way to start a Saturday.

Animals!

The tears stung my eyes. I felt at least a hundred years old.

The phone had woken me at ten, requested my attendance at the infirmary.

Well, here I was, and now the tears had begun to drip from my chin.

She looked as old as I felt, and that was decrepit. One half of her face was swollen, the other half covered in bandages, lips bloodless.

Superficial injuries, the doctors assured me, no broken bones. But stuff doctors! What the hell do they know! My knee began to ache at the memory, bear testimony to their expertise.

And why had those animals hurt this old woman? This old woman who had suffered so much pain and misery in her life—why her!

And I was doing okay, I told myself sourly. I'd totted up my score to three. The barman, Sharon Walsh, and now Mrs Harker.

'Don't take on so, Frankie,' she was mumbling, voice strained. 'I'm fine. I'll be up in a couple of days, you'll see. It takes more than a couple of scallywags to keep Mary Harker down.'

Scallywags! Two animals had beaten hell out of her and she referred to them as

119

scallywags. Jesus wept! My love and respect deepened.

She breathed painfully, tried to control the pain that rippled through her body. I took her hand in mine as it lay across the bed. My voice remained choked as I asked her to describe her attackers.

'I told your friend Kevin Bell the truth.' She shook her head slightly. 'It happened so quick I didn't really see them. Early this morning there was a knock on the door. I got out of bed to answer it.' There was the hint of a dry smile at the back of her eyes. 'I thought it was you, that you were drunk, or you'd lost your key again. I was grumbling as I came down the stairs. Next I knew I was hit in the face. I lied to Kevin after that. I said they were two young lads after money. They weren't. Grown men, that I do know.'

'And they wanted me?'

'Not exactly. They gave me a message for you. They said this was a sample of what to expect. They said you were to keep your nose out of their business. They said you'd understand. That's why I lied to Kevin—for you.' There was an appeal in her voice. 'Do as they say, Frankie.'

She was a tough old bird in many ways; a survivor who hadn't been soured. I squeezed her dry palm to express the affection I could never put into words.

But nothing could stop me now. I'd nail the

bastards. I'd maim them. Curly and Mute, and the man behind them, who I believed to be a certain Jack Evans. I felt a fierce determination that was new to me. I knew I'd come through this.

And anyway, there was no way out for me. What they had done to Mrs Harker was more than a warning, it was pure animal viciousness because I had made fools of them. They had hurt the only person I was really close to. And hell, they still wanted me—probably more than ever. It was simply that they had changed tactics for a while.

'Okay, I'll lay off,' I said, forcing a smile that didn't quite work.

I wasn't fooling her and we both knew it. Her old eyes pierced mine. I stood quickly before she could speak. My voice was thick in my tight throat.

'And stop coming the old martyr. I want you out of that bed tomorrow. You're just a skiving old biddy trying to get out of knitting my pullover. And it's nearly Christmas.'

I stormed out, feet slamming on the tiles of the corridor, eager to be gone from the stink of blood and antiseptic. I only made ten strides. He sat on the hard bench by the wall, smoking casually despite the multitude of lethal warnings around him. With his knuckles he rapped the place beside him and stretched his legs.

'Sit—Frankie,' he said quietly.

121

'Go toss yourself off!'

Another five strides and the edge in his voice stopped me stone dead.

'I'm not asking, Frankie!'

Faces turned our way, looked nervous, unsure how to react. A pink cheeked nurse with all the bravado of youth made a move towards us then changed her mind as Kevin Bell's eyes scorched her. She contented herself by clucking her tongue and shaking a sad head. I shrugged, and flopped down next to him.

His voice was hushed again, matching his surroundings. 'Tell me what this is about, Frankie.'

'None of your business,' I retorted churlishly.

He pointed to a door. 'The beating of that old woman makes it my business.' He paused. 'I'm fond of her too.'

Maybe he was. But this was personal. He hadn't mentioned the assault on the barman. Which meant the boy hadn't spoken, tied my name in. I wasn't surprised he hadn't told the police the truth. Sharon Walsh hadn't even taken her pains to a hospital, she nursed herself in the silence and fear of her own flat.

'They were nothing more than a couple of yobs scratching for money,' I said.

'Pull the other—it has bells.' He made a dismissive noise in his throat. 'Mrs Harker lied. I know that. Does this concern Karen Richardson—have you found her?'

'No,' I replied truthfully.

There was a long silence. Kevin seemed to be chewing on something at the back of his mind.

'The name you gave me over the phone the other day—Eddie Morgan. As I told you, the name sounded familiar. Next day I checked. He originates from Bolton. Something of a tearaway in his younger days. He died last weekend.'

'An accident, I presume,' I commented drily.

'That's right. There was talk that another car might be involved. It came to nothing. I checked with the locals. Morgan was pissed to the gills.' He studied me. 'You know all this?' I nodded. 'Did you know that we pulled Morgan in about a year ago?' It was news to me. My ears pricked, but I soon lost interest. 'The usual stuff for him. Using his fists. I never met him personally. The gist is, he got off with a fine.'

'You don't say,' I commented, bored.

'I do.' He sighed. 'So what is your interest in Eddie Morgan?'

'He was a friend of Karen's.'

'A strange pairing.' He took a last drag and ground out the cigarette under his heel. 'What were they up to—ignoring the obvious?'

'The obvious never took place!' I snapped. I decided to give him a little of the truth. 'Karen was a junkie.' I glanced at him to gauge his reaction. I caught just a glimmer of interest before it disappeared. 'Morgan supplied her.'

'Sounds likely.' He showed no surprise on that point. 'Are you thinking there is a connection between her disappearance and Morgan's death?'

'I think it possible,' I said wearily. I changed tack.

'Know a bloke named Jimmy Keegan?'

'By reputation.' He smiled. 'Brother-in-law of Jack Evans, the brother of Evans's ex-wife. A lot younger than his sister, and when the marriage didn't produce offspring he became more of an adopted son. After they split Jimmy stayed on at Jack's place. Apparently he thinks the sun shines out of Jack's backside.'

That answered a lot of questions. 'Does Keegan deal in drugs?'

That made Kevin sit up. 'I've never heard it whispered, and I'd be poleaxed if it were true. Jack is strictly legit these days. If he thought Keegan was playing around the drug scene I have the notion Jack would skin him. Is there a connection between Keegan and Morgan?'

I shrugged. I'd said enough to Kevin, maybe too much. I stood. But Kevin wasn't through. He gripped my elbow.

'I still don't know what you're into, Frankie, but I'm interested now. I'm giving you twenty-four hours, then I'll come looking for you. And you'll talk. Whatever is happening, I'm going to clear it up. I don't like drugs, I don't like talk of drugs. Understand me?'

I understood all right. Kevin had the sniff of the glory trail in his nostrils.

*　　　*　　　*

I went the back way to make sure I wasn't spotted. My knock was answered by a middle-aged woman. I claimed to be a friend of Terry's, and had called to see how he was making out. She pointed me to the front room.

Terry, the barman from Raven's, sat on an easy chair, a newspaper open on his knee. His skin was very pale but for a discoloration on his jaw.

There was no hostility in his eyes. I relaxed, took a seat on the sofa. He was still able to smile.

'I sure as hell earned that pound.' His head shook ruefully. 'And I hope nobody saw you enter, mate.'

'I came the back way,' I said, answering his smile. 'Want to talk about it?'

He talked, but made it plain whatever he said would never go beyond these walls. He had lied to the police once, and would do so again. The description of his attackers fitted Curly and Mute. He had repeated to them everything he had told me in Raven's. Yes, he had mentioned Sharon Walsh.

He had simply confirmed what I had already guessed. I wished him good health and a

125

speedy recovery.

*   *   *

'Look.' Irene Downes took a deep breath, angry with my tedious questions. 'So okay. I did know where Karen was heading for when she left here that Thursday night. And you are very clever.' She pulled an ironic face. 'I slipped up, okay? Of course she wouldn't ask me for forty pounds to buy drugs off Eddie. She had to have someone else in mind. I gave her the name of that someone else—Jimmy Keegan.'

I had inched forward another fraction. 'Keegan and Eddie were friends?'

'Not exactly. Eddie fawned on Keegan because he thought Keegan was something special, the big time he yearned for. Keegan called here once and showered us with his ego.' She paused. 'So Karen was here that night, and Eddie wasn't. I mentioned Keegan, saying that perhaps he might be able to help her. I was surprised when she said she knew him. Apparently she'd once worked at the Pit and met him there. She asked me for forty pounds. I didn't have it. But she was desperate enough to go to the Pit and try Keegan anyway. And that is the way it was—exactly.'

I believed her, up to there, but there was an even more important question; a wild shot that just might work.

126

'She came back, didn't she? Probably in the early hours of Friday morning?' No response, lips tight. 'She might be dead, Irenc. At the very least she is in danger. Help me.'

It took a long time for her to make up her mind, then Irene Downes began to wilt before my eyes. There was a soft centre to that hard shell she showed the world.

'Oh, God. They killed Eddie, didn't they? That's why I was scared to speak. I didn't believe you when you said Eddie died in an accident. It was too pat. I knew why he ran off. I knew why those men came looking for him. And God forgive me. I sent them after him. When you told me Eddie had died I didn't want to get involved. I was scared they'd come back and kill me.'

I didn't interrupt, let her reach her own decisions. Her voice had dropped very low and I had to strain my ears to pick out her words.

'Yes, Karen came back. Around two in the morning. She hammered on the door and Eddie got up to let her in. I didn't even see her. I stayed in bed. I knew there'd be a scene, a fight.'

'But you heard what passed between them?'

Her eyes said yes. 'She was hysterical, out of breath. She kept repeating stuff like, "Help me. They saw me. I know they'll kill me." I heard Eddie slap her. Then it went quiet for a while, and they began to talk softly. I crept to the door and listened.'

127

Irene lit a cigarette, and drew on it savagely. The room had gone very quiet.

'Karen was speaking in that little voice of hers. It didn't make complete sense to me. There was something about Jimmy cheating her, then falling asleep in a van. She was shivering when she awoke and the van was moving. She was on a mattress in the back. She sensed trouble and decided to keep quiet as they obviously didn't know she was there. There were two men in the front. One was Keegan.'

'And the other?' I asked eagerly, beginning to sweat as I sat on the edge of my seat.

'A big man. Balding. Jimmy referred to him as Jack.' I wiped my clammy palms, aware that I was coming close to solving the puzzle. 'They were discussing some men. Apparently, these men had taken enough crap from Jack and were through. Though through with what, I've no idea. They wanted their cut of the money and to be driven out of town. The big man was saying that according to the plan they should stay where they were until Saturday. He seemed to be blaming Jimmy. Jimmy was wriggling, saying he hadn't chosen the men. Karen was getting more frightened. She knew they'd damage her if they found her. Then the van pulled up. The two men got out. They stood there a few seconds then one of them cursed and they moved away.

'Karen peeked through the window. The

van was parked on waste ground. She could make out Jimmy and the big man in the darkness. They entered the end house of a derelict terrace, squeezing past a corrugated sheet that covered the door.

'Karen was puzzled, but even more terrified. She slipped from the van and began to creep away. She hadn't gone far when she heard voices. She crouched down by a wall. There were six men now, and they were moving towards the van. Something startled Karen, a spider, a mouse, and she stood up. One of the men saw her and pointed.

'He shouted, "Over there."

'They looked her way, but it was very dark. "A night bird taking a pee," the same voice laughed. But somebody shouted that they'd better grab her. Karen ran. Somebody was calling behind her, footsteps. She ducked down an alley and crawled into a doorway. Somebody ran past. Another man was calling in the distance. Then there was deep silence. She waited about an hour then made her way here.'

'The location of the terrace?' I demanded.

'Eddie asked her that. The Platting end of town, where they started to rip down the old terraces before they ran out of cash. Karen began to remember as Eddie questioned her. There was a slogan painted on the gable end. Beeler is queer. That's what it said.

'Eddie asked Karen if she'd been

recognised. She said no, but in my opinion only because the poor kid thought that was the answer Eddie wanted to hear. He believed her, more fool him. She wouldn't have been so scared if she thought they hadn't recognised her.'

There was a logic to that. I asked her to continue her story.

'Karen wanted Eddie to drive her out of town, or provide her with the money to leave. He wasn't having that. He told her to go home and keep her mouth shut, that there was nothing to worry about, that he'd take care of everything. She wasn't listening. He practically had to toss her out of the flat.

'He was whistling when he came back to bed. I pretended to be asleep. Whatever Karen had got herself mixed up in was now involving Eddie, and I just didn't want to know. Ignorance can be sweet.' Her eyes locked on mine. 'He tried something and it went wrong? They killed Eddie because of what Karen told him, didn't they?'

'It led to it,' I answered. 'His mistake was lack of intuition, and greed, and callousness. He deserved what he got, Irene. I feel nothing for Eddie Morgan.'

She didn't respond. She didn't even look at me as I left. I sat in my car, the window rolled down, lit a cigarette and puzzled.

So Karen was in that van with two men, only they didn't know it. Jimmy Keegan and a balding man named Jack, who was Jack Evans. And they talked of four restless men who wanted to be driven out of town, and more importantly—their cut of the money. So what money? The answer was plain, and it had nothing to do with drugs.

It was now time for me to pay a visit on my pal at the local newspaper.

CHAPTER THIRTEEN

Malcolm Fairhurst was tall and thin, all sharp corners and wet eyes. We had been in the same class at school and had remained good mates. He possessed an insatiable thirst for knowledge, no matter how trivial. With the job on the local newspaper he'd fallen into paradise.

I'd finally drawn him round to the wages snatch at the Motor Works.

'Very neat,' he was saying. I settled back. Malcolm never used one word when he could scratch along with twenty. 'But we've got to go back a little. Friday, the twenty-seventh, and the van from the company that supplies and launders the overalls for the factory is stopped. The driver is tied up, gagged, and rolled into a ditch.

'Okay. The van proceeds to make the delivery. No problem at the security gate. The driver has the right credentials, even if he is a new face. He drives to the storeroom where the overalls are stacked ready for distribution. Now this just happens to be close to the wages office. The driver gets out and begins to unload the sacks.

'Nobody sees the three men come from the back of the van and burst into the small ante-room where the money is kept until it is passed into the main wages office to be made into packets. The head clerk and two security guards are there, and they are quickly dealt with. You don't argue with masked men carrying shotguns. They are being tied and the villains are ready to leave. Then the unexpected happens. A girl pops her head around the door that leads to the main wages office. She intends to ask the guards if they would like a cup of tea. Instead, she screams. One of the guns is fired. Luckily, the shot goes over the girl's head. But the alarm is punched and all hell breaks loose.

'The villains are quickly back in the van with the money. They crash through the security barrier. The police are already on their way. In a sidestreet the villains switch vehicles. The laundry van is found only minutes later. But nobody has seen the vehicle they switched to. It simply disappeared.

'There was some doubt as to whether they made it out of town. The route to the motorway network was quickly sealed off, as within minutes were all the minor roads. There was an intensive search of all vehicles. For a while the theory was that the villains were still here. The police turned the town upside down. They found nothing. Now they seem to accept that somehow the villains made it through the cordon.

'Not long after the robbery there was an anonymous call to this office giving details of where to find the original driver of the laundry van. We passed the message on.'

I asked if the men could have been local.

'Unlikely. The local villains were pulled in—and nothing. There would have been a whisper of some sort. No, they were outsiders.'

I side-tracked him for a while; sex and football, his favourite topics. Then, I slipped in, 'What do you know of Jack Evans?'

'You asked me to gen-up on him.' He whistled softly. 'But I probably know no more than you. Everybody in this part of the world knows about Jack.'

'But you have written articles on him?'

'That's true,' he said grandly. 'Jack is by far our biggest advertiser, so we give him a big write-up every so often—it's usually a load of bull.'

'So talk. Bull or not.'

'Okay.' He rested back. 'Jack was born in the Depression. Little formal education, but quite smart. Petty criminal, a hard man with his fists. Couple of minor arrests. Then he decided to try something different.

'Nothing big. He started with a protection racket, corner shops and pubs. A few quid here and there. It didn't last long. Somebody laughed in his face and told him to go to hell. Jack lost his temper, and the bloke lost an eye. Jack spent the next four years behind bars.

'He wised up, as the Yanks say. He came out and began his own clothing business. He soon had an army of women sewing in their homes for pin money. Eventually, he got hold of a couple of run-down mills on the cheap, and he never looked back. He became quite a lad in the rag trade. He still lives local—a lovely house in a quiet village just outside town. He revels in the role of squire.'

I asked if Jack had been involved in any criminal activities since he left prison. Malcolm's eyes had narrowed as he regarded me. I didn't like it.

'Not that I know of,' he said quietly, eyes becoming familiar slits. 'First you give me a tinkle asking who owns a couple of clubs, and I tell you Jack's ex-wife. You ask me to dig up information on Jack. Now, here you are, nosing after Jack—and digging into the business at the Motor Works. What's the score, Frankie?'

I shrugged negligently. I said it was just a whisper I had heard over a quiet pint. He obviously didn't believe me, but he didn't press. I asked what Jack was doing these days.

'The usual. Horses. He owns five now. Only last week he had a big winner at Haydock.'

My ears pricked. 'And he threw a celebration party?'

Malcolm's eyes remained fixed on my face. 'That is Jack's usual style.'

I asked if Jack let it be known he had a criminal record. Malcolm laughed.

'Sure he does. He saw the light and repented. He bores everybody with the tale of how he encountered God while serving time. A regular little church-goer is Jack.' He paused. 'He has good taste in women too. His number two hobby after racing. Doesn't have one living in though. No claims on Jack when he feels like a change. He lives in that house with his brother-in-law and a housekeeper cum cook. She's pushing seventy—and deaf.'

I asked if he knew the brother-in-law.

He shook his head. I described Curly and Mute and asked if he had ever come across them in connection with Jack. Again he shook his head.

I was on my feet. I was aware of his curious eyes in the middle of my back as I left.

I used a phone, got the housekeeper. She was indeed deaf. I shouted, finally got her to understand that I wanted to speak to Jimmy Keegan. But no luck. Jimmy was away. He'd been gone a week and she didn't know when he'd be back. I hung up.

It had taken less than ten minutes of driving in circles to find it. Row upon row of boarded windows and doors, dark patches of naked earth where some of the terraces had been ripped down. But the area was still inhabited, a monumental triumph to human endurance. Smoke curled from the occasional chimney. A few kids kicked footballs. Old people walked the pavements. Young women pushed prams.

BEELER IS QUEER

I didn't ponder too long on the identity of Beeler. I parked near the gable end of the terrace. The nameplate read Harper Street. I studied the muddy earth for signs of tyre tracks, and of course there were none. The heavens had opened since Jimmy Keegan brought his van to this very spot, Karen cringing in the back.

I pulled my jacket tight and moved to the doorway. I squeezed past the corrugated sheet as other men had done.

Hard to believe that a family had once lived here. Water ran down the walls, the fireplace filled with rubble. The place stank of doom and decay.

No sign of recent occupation on the ground floor. I moved upstairs, careful of the rotting boards, pressing close to the damp walls.

Creaking doors, ghostly bedrooms, shattered windows, plaster hanging in sheets from above. My nerves became just a little frayed.

Still nothing.

I made a stack of what odds and ends I could find and balanced on them. I punched open the hatch to the attic and squirmed inside. It was hard going. My arms ached. I cursed my lack of condition, my spreading belly. But at last I was inside.

I was staring down the length of the terrace, like some great empty burial chamber. Light slanted in through gaps in the roof. I moved carefully, aware that a slip might send me plummeting to the bedrooms below. I soon found what I wanted. The men hadn't bothered to clean it out thoroughly.

They had built themselves a nest, collected planking to make the floor more solid. There were discarded tins and blankets, a shattered thermos flask.

I'd seen enough. I clambered back through the hatch and down the stairs. Only when I was outside did I spot the ladder they had used to reach the attic, tossed aside in the grass and mud.

I took time out to think.

The attic had been used as a hideout after the wages snatch. The men were supposed to stay for nine days, Friday to Saturday week. They only made it to the seventh day. They grew bored with living like animals. Around midnight of that fateful Thursday one of them came downstairs. He made a phone call. I cast my eyes around and, in the distance, forlorn and standing sentinel at a crossroads, I saw the phone box he had probably used. Evans had to act. He decided to bring the men out. With the faithful Keegan he came to collect them in the van. And then there was Karen.

Did Keegan recognise her?

I wondered. If he had, the search for Karen should have started much sooner. They chased her from this spot, then gave up. The real search only began the following afternoon, probably after the intervention of Eddie Morgan.

I tramped the area. I knocked on the doors of the inhabited houses, received varying reactions; from indifference to anger. Maybe it was me, my sour face, my overt aggression. But in an area such as this, questions meant trouble, the police.

'Did you see a vehicle in the vicinity of Harper Street on the morning of the twenty-sixth of November?'

No luck, try elsewhere, a slammed door. I finally struck lucky with a pair of scruffy, and very nosy young females.

'Sure. A van. Dunno what time. Yeah, near Harper Street. Some men in overalls. I asked one if he had a spare fag and he told me to bugger off. They came in a council van, something about getting ready to knock the houses down. The van? Red and white thing with the name of the town down the side. Dunno, didn't see where it went.'

I asked if they would recognise the men if they saw them again. Sure they would, the man they spoke to anyway. I found the description of this man very interesting. I took their names, and tipped them a fag each. Contributing to the delinquency of a minor— but who the hell cared. I was soon in a phone box and talking to Kevin.

'The area where the laundry van was dumped,' I was saying. 'You obviously enquired about other vehicles in the vicinity— did anyone mention a council van?'

A long pause, and I could almost hear the pulse of his brain. 'If I remember rightly—yes.'

Which meant most definitely. 'Did you follow it up?'

'Need you ask. All accounted for.'

I sniggered. 'Think so, mate?'

'Talk, Frankie!'

'Eat your heart out!'

I hung up, grinning.

Some people might think Kevin would come looking for me like the good little policeman he was—but I knew different. Kevin was a bright lad, brain as sharp as ginger. He wouldn't press me. He'd wait, patient as ever; or at the very least, he'd allow me those promised twenty-four hours.

CHAPTER FOURTEEN

I killed time in the Forger, drank a little too much, and almost allowed myself to be dragged into a fight that didn't concern me. Around ten I slipped quietly through the back door. I made sure I wasn't followed.

Half an hour later I was thumbing the bell to Anne Lindsay's flat. A full minute passed and no response. I hadn't expected one. At this moment she would be doing her stuff at Raven's—thrilling the voyeurs.

I slipped the freshly cut key into the lock and twisted. I stepped quietly inside. I waited until my eyes had adjusted to the light before I began to explore.

There were male clothes in the wardrobe, shirts, socks, a quiet business suit which from the size I guessed belonged to Jack Evans.

I sprung open the lock on the writing desk with my penknife, and switched on the small reading lamp. The room turned eerie in the soft glow. I found photographs of Anne and Jack. I dug deeper. From the back I pulled out a bundle of letters and a single photograph.

I leaned back, smiling as I studied the photograph.

Right enough, there was another man in Anne's life beside Jack. He was young, probably still in his twenties, and very handsome.

The letters had a tale to tell. Very graphic they were. It seemed that Jack kept Anne, and Anne kept this young man, using Jack's money to finance his various and unsuccessful business enterprises. The letters crooned about love and marriage and a bright future.

I slipped the bundle into my pocket, knocked off the light, and found myself a roomy airing cupboard to hide and wait.

She arrived less than an hour later. I heard voices. For a few moments my heart beat madly. Then I heard a muted goodbye. She entered alone.

I relaxed, happy to have been proved right. Jack had given her a bodyguard to see her to her door. It meant Jack was scared of me. I liked that.

I listened to her movements. I heard the refrigerator door, the clink of ice cubes. I slipped out and settled in the swing chair in the living room. I watched her enter, move to the stereo, sip from the glass in her hand.

'Hi, sweetheart,' I said quietly, in my best American drawl.

She swung round, spilling liquid over her dress. Her jaw hung slackly, then she grabbed for the telephone. I laughed, waved the bundle of letters.

'When you're through pass the phone to me and I'll render Jack a few choice extracts from these.'

A moment's pause and she dropped the receiver. Her eyes cut into me like fiery diamonds.

'How the hell did you get in here!' she hissed.

'Trade secret.' I winked. 'Where do I find Jimmy Keegan?'

'I don't know!' She glared, challenging. 'He lives with Jack. If he's not there—up yours!'

She was a real lady. I shrugged, shuffled the letters. 'I'd like to be a fly on the wall when Jack reads these.' I clucked my tongue. 'He won't be happy, sweetheart, giving you expensive presents and you passing them on to your boyfriend.' I sighed. 'And an old friend of mine was beaten up this morning—and I'm not happy about that.'

Some of the rage slipped from her face. She relaxed. She flopped into the seat opposite, her short skirt hitched around her thighs.

'What do you want?' she asked softly.

'First—Keegan.'

'Westfield nursing home,' she said quickly. 'He was a naughty boy. It earned him a beating with a cricket bat. I don't know the details, or just what he did. It was something Jack let slip.'

It figured. Jack might take a cricket bat to Keegan, but from there on it would be the five-star hospital treatment.

'How much were you paid to set me up?' I asked.

Silence for a while, then she smiled maliciously. 'Nothing. You came to Raven's and mentioned Karen Richardson. I knew Jack was interested in her. I rang him and he told me to bring you here and keep you occupied while he organised a couple of blokes to pick you up.'

'Who were the two blokes?'

'I don't know.' She folded her arms. 'That is all I am prepared to say.'

'I'm going to make a deal with you, sweetheart,' I said. 'When I walk from this flat, I'm going to give you enough time to pack, and sling your hook out of this town.'

'What is that—?'

'Shut it!' I snapped, cooled. 'We are discussing armed robbery. Unless you want to be involved, be a good girl and answer my questions. Think what prison will mean. Five years at least. When you come out your tits will already have begun to sag.'

She thought. Hell! How she thought. The warm glow from her ticking brain raised the temperature of the room. Again I asked for the identity of the two men who tried to snatch me from this flat.

'Friends of Jack's,' she said finally. 'I don't know their names—that's the truth. I first saw them a couple of days ago at the house. We didn't speak.'

Probably a lie, but I let it pass. 'What did they have in mind for me?'

Suddenly, her smile disconcerted me. She now seemed more amused than scared. 'Who cares.'

I resisted the urge to slap her. She had begun to lean forward and massage her calf as if she had cramp. A pink tongue moistened her lips. I tried to keep my mind elsewhere. I asked why Jack was so interested in Karen Richardson.

'Oh, I think you already know. I think you know most of the answers.' Her eyes held mine but I didn't respond. She shrugged. 'She heard something she wasn't supposed to.'

'Tell me about the night of the party.'

'Okay.' Still smiling, she leaned back, legs stretched. 'I was working. Then the mighty Keegan appears. Jack has had a winner and there is to be a party at his place. I have been summoned. I trot off with Keegan. He picks up a couple of girls at a table to take along. One was the Richardson girl. She was a pain in the arse. A heroin freak in search of a fix. Keegan said he'd sort her out. That was it. When we got to the house Keegan stayed in the van with the girl. The party was the usual drag.'

'And Jack left around midnight?' I asked.

'Apparently. I didn't see him go, but I was made aware of his return. He was in a foul temper. He took it out on me. My back was in strips the next day.'

'And he told you what he'd been doing?'

'Not then. But I picked up enough details over the next couple of hours. Jack is very talkative in bed.'

A few more questions, then I asked what else she did for Jack, discounting his regular joy rides.

'What do you think?' She laughed. 'Nothing for nothing in this world. I sometimes entertain his business friends.'

'You knew Keegan pushed drugs?'

'Not until that night, and even then I thought he was playing the Richardson girl along so he could get inside her pants.'

'Did Jack suspect Keegan of dealing?'

'Unlikely.' She smiled smugly. 'He once said that if he ever found one of his people on drugs, he'd break their legs. Seems there is a strong possibility he meant it.'

'Are you saying that is why he had Keegan hurt? Because he meddled in drugs, not because he left Karen in the back of that van?'

She shrugged. 'Probably a bit of both.'

The smile never left her face as she watched me move to the door. I was the lowest form of life in her eyes. But what the hell! She was nothing.

And she wouldn't mention my visit to Jack, she wouldn't telephone him. She'd said too much, and the letters in my pocket were another guarantee of her silence. And anyway, the day of Jack Evans was almost over, and she was smart enough to see it. When she'd had time to consider she'd realise nobody could tie her into the robbery. She was probably no more than an indifferent witness to the planning. But she'd run as soon as I left here. She'd only feel safe when Jack was behind bars. I knew where she'd run to.

I took one last look at her and wondered how something so beautiful could be so rotten.

*   *   *

Much the same opening as the day before. But Sunday wasn't such a bad day for hospital visiting. God was in the air, though he seemed to have given this room a miss. I'd conned my way in at this early hour by claiming to be a relative who later in the day would be on his way to the sunnier climes of South Africa.

And this was the fourth 'accident' victim I'd viewed lately, though this one I felt little pity for.

We'd talked this way and that for an hour, inching forward, inching back. I found Jimmy Keegan a particularly unloveable and pathetic character.

I'd given him my version of the wages snatch. With his leg in traction he looked very sorry for himself, and very perturbed. From time to time he eyed the telephone at the side of the bed. He knew he was in trouble if he even twitched a finger towards it. I used the clinching argument I hoped wouldn't turn out

146

to be fact.

'They murdered her, Jimmy. They killed Karen, Jimmy. Little Karen is dead—and you are involved. You'll go down with them.'

There was fear in his eyes, a naked touch of terror. He sweated, wiped his palms.

'From the beginning.' I struggled to keep the steel in my voice. 'I'll start it off for you. You are at the races. Jack has a big winner. He decides to celebrate. He is surrounded by his usual camp followers.' I paused. 'Take up the story, Jimmy.'

He swallowed, and the words began to dribble from his lips, gradually speeding up.

'We went to Jack's place. We'd already had quite a lot to drink and picked up a fair number of birds along the way. But Jack asked me to nip over to Raven's and collect Anne Lindsay.' He almost spat her name. 'She's an uppity, high strung cow! I got her. While I was there I came across two birds. One was a shagbag named Sharon. The other I hardly recognised. Karen. I remembered her from the Pit. I fancied her then but never got close. But surprise, surprise, she was looking for me. And you know why. I promised to see she was taken care of and took her along.

'We got to Jack's place and got into the back of the van. I'd never met such a useless piece. Her face screwed up and body as stiff as a board. We didn't even make it. She started to cry and act up, said it wasn't her fault if I'd

147

changed her mind, said I'd promised.

'So I had. But there was nothing I could do. I'm no pusher. I just do the odd favour for a pal.'

That might be true, but it bore an uncanny similarity to how someone had once described the late Eddie Morgan.

'But she kept bleating,' Keegan went on. 'I got cheesed off. I had no stuff on me, and there was certainly none in the house. I promised to take care of her first thing in the morning. And I meant it. I told her to tidy herself up and come inside. There was plenty of booze to make her forget. I left her in the van.

'I didn't see her after that. The party was swinging along fine then the phone rings. One of the bastards had left the hiding place. There'd been an argument. They wanted Jack to pick them up and drive them away—personally. Christ! That made Jack mad. Only one of the men was supposed to know his name, and it wasn't the bleeder using the phone. They insisted on Jack. Hell! Either he came for them, or they'd ring for a bloody taxi and come round to his place to collect the money. And the house was crowded and there was no way we could get rid of the guests. Jack had no option. I hadn't known about the robbery until then. But Jack insisted I come along.'

Keegan had begun to lie. His description

fitted the one given to me by the two girls in Harper Street. But I didn't contradict, allowed his words to flow.

'We went in my van. They didn't respond when we drove up. So we went inside the house. They were waiting. It was just after we left that I spotted the girl. She sort of jumped up from a crouching position. One of the men made a cheap crack.

'It was dark, but I recognised her. I knew how she'd got there. Christ! I nearly wet myself. I ran after her, and one of the other blokes did the same. The others thought we'd gone mad. I certainly had. I should have done nothing. God knows what I'd have done if I'd caught her. But she slipped us. I didn't say anything to Jack. The kid was a junkie. She wouldn't understand what she saw and heard. I forgot her. Jack paid the blokes and we dropped them on the outskirts of Manchester.

'Next day Morgan dropped me in the shit. I had no idea he even knew the girl. Then it struck me why she had come to me in search of a fix—Morgan must have mentioned me. I'd thought she'd simply heard a rumour while she worked at the Pit. So it's about lunch-time when Morgan rings Jack.'

'Blackmail?'

'Not quite. Morgan is a crawler, and decides that to crawl a little closer to Jack will do him some good. He wanted Jack to owe him. Anyway, that's how he had it figured. He was going to give Jack Karen Richardson's name, offer to keep her mouth shut.

'So Jack listens. His face gets dark with rage but he keeps his voice flat. He tells Morgan to come over to the house for a chat. Jack then recounts to me what's happened. The girl we spotted near the terrace had hitched a ride in the van—only we didn't know it. And we'd talked on that journey. We'd mentioned names and places.

'Jack wasn't happy. I was shitless. I knew once it came out who the girl was and how she'd come to be in the van he'd take me apart. I made an excuse to leave and headed Morgan off at the top of the lane.

'I told him Jack had a couple of heavies waiting at the house. I said Jack didn't like blackmailers. That they meant to bury him and the girl—deep. Morgan argued the toss, claimed he was doing Jack a favour. I made him see it different. I convinced him to clear out of town before Jack's boys came looking for him. I was warning him as a pal, and wouldn't go along with murder—even for Jack. Morgan was prick enough to believe me.

'But he wasn't the only prick. There was me. Morgan didn't turn up at the house and Jack grew restless. Then the Lindsay bitch strolled in. She gets the drift of the conversation. She asks what happened to the bird I had in the van, the little junkie—and had I fixed her up with a shot. She smirked as she said it. It all fell into place for Jack.

'And I could never stand up to Jack.' He glanced bitterly at his suspended leg. 'He did this. Bastard! He made me beg and still he did it.' He swallowed. 'He decided to bring in some outside help to apply the frighteners. But they couldn't find Morgan and the girl. They were running scared, but not scared enough for Jack. He wanted to make sure they stayed dumb. And it wouldn't have mattered if I hadn't headed Morgan off. Jack would still have put the frighteners on. Anyway, sometime later they might reappear and put the black on him, or they might talk to a third party. That was the big danger.'

'Who was the outside help?' I still hadn't put names to Curly and Mute.

'No idea. I never met them. I was already out of circulation. I've lived on rumours since. I heard they caught up with Morgan and he rammed his car into a tree. I didn't know they'd tracked down the girl.'

'The names of the four men on the wages snatch,' I demanded.

'Still no idea. Jack mentioned them that night in the van, but I've forgotten. It was the only time I saw them.'

A lie, but I was suddenly too weary to press. I had heard enough. Keegan watched me carefully as I stood.

'If the girl is dead—I had nothing to do with it. And, mate. I've said nothing to you.'

151

It was a final touch of bravado, and added up to nothing. He'd talk to the police when they came, and it would be the complete truth, not this barely thought out stew of half-truths he had given me.

CHAPTER FIFTEEN

I parked the car half a mile away, and walked. The day was grey, misty with drizzle. I cut across Tipping Wood where no lovers strolled hand in hand on a day such as this. I reached the house, glanced around. I saw nobody, not even a cat or dog. I quickly scaled the wall at the side and worked around to the front where I crouched in the bushes. I hoped the housekeeper was busy with the Sunday lunch in the kitchen.

I waited.

The car purred gently, swept through the open gate, braked. The garage door rose magically at the push of an unseen electronic button. The car disappeared. Only the driver inside, no Keegan to do the chauffeuring now.

I stepped out of hiding and strode quickly across the open ground to the garage. There were three cars inside, the light even murkier than that of the miserable day outside. The figure slammed the car door and turned. He saw me and stopped in his tracks a moment.

Then he moved forward a little, but made no move to pass. His bulk seemed to tower over me, but I felt no fear, just the odd twinge in my knee to keep my nerves on edge.

'You're trespassing, old son,' the voice barked.

'That's right, Jack.' My voice was cool, very cool.

He took a step closer, eyes narrowing in the dim light.

I detected his after-shave lotion, even knew the brand. The Bible gripped in his left hand infuriated me, mocked. God should have no place in the life of this man. I remembered Mrs Harker and my rage intensified.

'Do I know you, old son!' The same tone of voice.

'You should, Jack,' I said. 'I'm the man who shagged your girlfriend. I have to thank you for that at least. I also had a couple of misadventures with your thugs. They beat up an old woman I'm fond of. I'm not happy about that, or the trail of misery you've left. I'm here to settle the score.'

There was the glint of teeth as he smiled acidly. He came closer and only a few icy feet separated us. His breath smelled of peppermint.

'You're not big enough, old son! I once saw you play rugby. You were quick and sharp, but you lacked guts. You'd never have made it. I should have dealt with you myself instead of all this farting about. I'm going to break your back, old son.'

'You're nothing without your cricket bat, Jack.' I summoned a snigger. 'You're too old and fat. You probably can't even keep your pecker up for more than ten seconds.' Still I hadn't got through to him. 'I've been talking to Anne Lindsay and Jimmy Keegan—you're going back inside. Maybe you'll find a pretty boy to amuse you.'

He came at me with the roar of a bull. And I was right—he was too old, and too fat. I lashed him in the crotch before he reached me. He was down, puking on the dark concrete, and I shoved his face into the mess he made. I hit him once more flush on the nose.

'The girl, Jack!' I rasped. 'Karen! Where is she!'

He pushed to his elbows, strained for breath. 'When I learn the answer to that, old son, I'll skin her and stitch her hide to your mouth.'

My fist pulled back, and stayed there. And somehow it didn't matter any more. I was no thug. I left him there, in his own filth.

I stopped at the first phone box. I was soon mad, sweating. Kevin wasn't in his office, or at home. I rang around frantically. It took almost half an hour to track him down. I told him about the house in Harper Street, Jimmy Keegan, everything I knew. I replaced the receiver.

I made myself scarce for a while, I needed time to think, set my mind in logical order.

*   *   *

The early hours of Tuesday.

Forty hours had passed, my head ached. I felt no sense of triumph. I felt hollow and disillusioned.

Kevin lolled back behind his desk, fingers locked behind his head. He said casually, 'Jack Evans claims he was assaulted on his way home from church.'

'Oh.' I affected an air of innocence. 'Who by?'

'He isn't saying.' His eyes locked on mine. 'He says it's personal. And though Jack's going down for a long time, if I were that bloke I'd tread carefully.'

'Nothing to do with me.' I yawned. 'So how has it gone?'

'Like a ripe peach.' He made a ring of his finger and thumb. 'We took the attic in Harper Street apart. We got several juicy prints off the cans they left, a smear of blood where one of the clowns cut himself. We already have them. Picked them up in Manchester. Amateurs but for one. A man named Mason. He served time with Jack in the days of the Ark. They kept in touch.

'We've also been delving into Jack's business empire. And very shaky it turned out

155

to be. His world was disintegrating. He needed cash, and quick. He was preparing to cut and run before the fraud boys moved in. Jack's idea of oiling the wheels of commerce was to fork out a hefty bribe. He was already negotiating the sale of his house and horses.

'Sunday morning the process was speeded up. We picked him up at Manchester Airport, booked on a flight to Miami. From there who knows where he intended to disappear to.'

I smiled secretly, smugly. I thought Jack might run after the confrontation with me. In fact, I knew. I wanted that extra nail in his coffin. I could picture the scene after I left him. Jack enters the house, picks up the phone. No response from Anne Lindsay's flat. A call to Keegan, who probably stuttered into the phone for a few seconds then hung up. Yes, Jack had to run.

'Keegan's done most of the talking,' Kevin went on. 'He set the ball rolling for the caper at the Motor Works. He met a clerk from the wages office and mentioned it to Jack. The clerk was soon bought and paid for. We have him. So Jack needed cash and that's how it began. He got in touch with Mason, who put the team together. It was a mistake. Mason was way past his best. There was no way he could control the young bucks he chose.

'The snatch itself went sweetly enough, until the girl walked in on them. But they made it to the first changeover. They left the van, down an alley, and into the council van that was waiting in the next street.

'But we moved too quickly. Not many routes out of this town, and it was soon sealed off. Within minutes of the snatch they should have been on the motorway heading south, then pulling off at the first interchange where a car was waiting. They were monitoring our movements by radio, so they knew this wasn't on. Wearing overalls and in that van they might have bluffed their way through. But their faces would have been remembered. Only the lad who had driven the laundry van into the factory had no previous form, a face that couldn't be fingered in a file. So they decided on the contingency plan and drove to Harper Street.

'It was ill conceived. The attic was for an emergency they thought would never happen. They hadn't given it enough thought. All they had were a few cans and flasks, no contact with anyone outside. And the weather was particularly foul. Three days would have been sufficient. But Jack had planned for ten. And he meant to stick by it.

'They were to have mingled with the football crowd as it left the stadium on the Saturday afternoon, a car waiting with their cut of money in the boot. But they grew restless, and worried. For all they knew they might have been double-crossed. The tension increased. The three younger men began to put pressure on Mason. He couldn't control them. He gave them Jack's name. So one of them left the attic to telephone him, insist he come personally to drive them away, and bring the money.

'They wanted Jack involved of course. They didn't know him, so they didn't trust him. They wanted him to know that if anything went wrong they'd take him down with them. They were a bunch of yobs exercising a little power, and repaying Jack for the lost days they spent in that attic.

'And Keegan was in it up to his neck. He procured the council van, and drove it. He took them to Harper Street. He dropped them off and took the haul to Jack.

'So Jack was blackmailed into picking up his little gang, and it would have been okay but for the sleeping girl in the back. And Jack was never connected with the clubs. A lot of people thought he was, and he let them think that way. It did no harm to his image. No. The clubs always belonged to Doreen Evans. Her managers had instructions to humour and suffer her little brother Jimmy. She owns seven clubs now. Their rise coincided with Jack's fall. He kept up a good front, maintained his lifestyle, his horses and women, but it had turned sour. He even tried to get financial help from Doreen. She refused.'

'Curly and Mute, the old lady?'

'Business associates of Jack that he's used

158

occasionally. A Liverpool firm. Basically the same line of work as you—only heavier. Mainly the rougher end of the debt collecting business, and that's what Jack had used them for in the past. The old lady is the boss, and the mother of Mute, as you christened him. A sweet old soul. Jack brought her in to find Morgan and the girl, and the price was high because along the way she was sure to suss out Jack's involvement with the wages snatch. It was a chance he was willing to take.

'Obviously nobody is saying what they had in mind for the missing duo. But my guess is they only meant to scare them, inflict a little damage. They found Morgan. Blind drunk he wrapped his car around a tree when they pulled their cowboy stunt. After the business with Mrs Harker the old lady pulled her boys out. She knew it was getting out of hand.'

'How did they get on to me?' I asked.

'Curly had the feeling that Karen might be hiding in the Spencer house. They didn't attempt any rough stuff though. The old lady was watching the house when you showed up. From curiosity she followed you. It didn't take long to discover your trade and what you were working on. She did the tagging for the first couple of days, before she almost walked into your arms.

'Curly and Mute took over next day and tried to run you off the road. After that they gave you a day's breather, before the old lady

159

took over again. They knew you were getting close, and were growing a little desperate. Once you had got on to Eddie Morgan, Jack told them to shake you up a little. I think they intended to break your legs, old mate.'

I shuddered. 'So what are you booking them on?'

'Assault. The barman from Raven's and Sharon Walsh are now willing to give evidence. Mrs Harker can't identify them—so that's out, and we'll never be able to tie them into Morgan's death, and they never actually claimed to be police officers. They say Jack Evans hired them to run to earth a couple of bad debtors and along the way they became a little over-zealous.'

'Anne Lindsay?'

'Found her where you said. With her boyfriend.' He grinned. 'She's cursing you. She'll give evidence and she won't be charged with complicity. She'll walk from the court laughing.'

'Jimmy Keegan and the drugs?'

'He gave you the truth. He was no higher on that scene than Eddie Morgan. Two little soul brothers those two. He did a little minor dealing. He was a smart arse who thought it made him a big man. We have a name and we'll follow it through.'

'And Karen?' I asked reluctantly.

'They never found her. That's the plain fact.'

I already knew. I'd reached the same conclusion in those long hours I'd spent alone after I left Jack Evans. They were still hunting her when I first appeared. Okay, they could have found her since, disposed of her—but it was never on. They tried to eliminate me to stop me getting to Karen before themselves, not to cover up her murder. A stab of rage and helplessness shot through me.

'So where is she!'

'I don't know,' Kevin replied. 'But we want her now. We'll find her. Anyway, once she hears we have Jack Evans—she'll emerge.'

His indifference infuriated me. 'You still haven't answered my question!'

'Oh, I thought I had.' His eyes were quizzical. 'She's with a bloke, old mate. A boyfriend you never found.'

He still hadn't understood. I still hadn't got him to understand the complexity of Karen's character. There was no boyfriend. It was useless to press on. I didn't linger. I needed fresh air.

CHAPTER SIXTEEN

Wednesday morning; yellow light illuminated the office from the pale sun that turned low in a clear blue sky. It did nothing to raise my spirits.

Still no Karen.

She must have heard that Evans was in custody. So why hadn't she come forward?

Still afraid of the police? The possibility of giving evidence at the trial? Perhaps. She had been through that harrowing experience before. It was an answer of sorts, but it didn't satisfy me.

Was Kevin right? Was she with a boyfriend I had failed to discover? I didn't think so. Men scared Karen, possibly revolted her. Certainly young men who entertained ideas of a sexual nature. Absurdly, Eddie Morgan was the only young man she felt comfortable with. She sensed no sexual danger from him. She amused him, and that was something new for her. She took to drugs happily, without consideration of the consequences. They were an escape to the land of dreams, a release for emotions that had stayed locked inside all her life.

I turned uneasily in my chair. I was getting nowhere with idle speculations. I was soon on the motorway and heading south for a conference with the Richardsons.

*   *   *

It was a lower middle-class suburb of detached houses, neat gardens, neat cars in the drive. The inside of the house was spotlessly clean, colours muted to match the personalities of

162

the occupants.

We travelled over old ground.

Twice more she recounted the nightmare, or vision, or whatever it was, and once again she almost had me believing. The shivers rippled over my skin and moistened my palms. She insisted that Karen had died at fourteen minutes past four on that Friday morning, and nothing could budge her.

Yes, the police had been to see her. Yesterday. A Detective Chief Inspector. Yes, she had recounted her experience to him. No, he obviously didn't believe it could be true. He was of the opinion that Karen was still alive, and hiding. She wished me to continue my search for her daughter.

I asked questions. I dug deeper into Karen's personality. The Richardsons looked to each other, communicated silently, and for the first time I noticed that Mr Richardson was a sick man, as had once been pointed out to me by Val Spencer. There was a greyness about him, the haunting sheen of death across his eyes. Mrs Richardson barely nodded and turned to me.

'Yes, Karen was a little unstable, particularly so after the rape. She threw tantrums and was often hard to control. But the tantrums died as quickly as they erupted, then it was as though nothing had happened. In the aftermath of the rape we explained this to the doctors. There was never any question of her bearing the

163

child, Mr Conroy. She was mentally unstable at the time. She wanted a new doll to play with. As simple as that. We denied her. It was unfair of her to blame her father. Her attitude was destroying them both. That's why we thought it best that she go to Val. They were always close. It seemed to have worked. She even got her own flat. She seemed to have become more independent.'

She dropped into silence. There was little more to be said.

*   *   *

I was back to square one. I did some deep thinking as I returned north. I went over those first couple of days before I became side-tracked by the wages snatch, the people I'd met and spoken to.

And now there was an itch at the back of my mind. Someone had said something, just a few simple words that came out in a casual conversation—but they were important.

But hell! I couldn't relieve that itch!

*   *   *

'Let the whole world hear!'

George Benson was no longer concerned with his dignity. He wasn't concerned with the inquisitive Thursday crowd we had gathered.

'It doesn't make sense, George!' I bawled

back.

'To you—maybe!' Some of the rage left his voice and he held up his hands in exasperation. 'We were friends—nothing more.'

And that would have to do, for now, but I'd be back for the truth. He conceded me the name of the hotel he had stayed at with Karen in the Lakes, and nothing more.

And where did people head when they wished to hide? Worldly people headed for the anonymity of the great cities. They could make out. People like Karen? They hid behind friends or relatives. But Karen had no friends. Her only relatives were a father and mother, and she wasn't with them. So how about familiar territory? The place she spent those weekends with George Benson? She had no money, but perhaps she thought she might be able to find casual work, waitress maybe. It was worth a shot.

I was back on the motorway. The sun still shone, the air crystal clear. I should have been happy to be alive—I wasn't.

*   *   *

The town was beautiful in the golden light, but no tourists thronged the pavements, just a few hardy ramblers with knapsacks on their backs.

Her blouse was crisp and white and matched her hair. Her smile clicked on and off as if manipulated by a string under the counter. Still, it was a pleasant enough smile. She wasn't averse to answering my questions.

Yes, a George Benson had stayed here regularly. A nice man, friendly without being familiar. He came with his daughter. My ears turned hot. Karen? Yes, that would be her name. She did quite a bit of sketching. No, she hadn't seen either of them for some months. No, the girl had not returned on her own. Sorry, she couldn't help me further.

I trekked around the town for some hours. I tried hotels, cafés, souvenir shops, those that were open in the off season. I even tried the Job Centre. Nobody remembered having seen Karen.

It had been a wasted journey.

*   *   *

Friday, the sun still shone.

Malcolm snapped a fresh roll into the camera. I nudged him in the ribs.

'Here he comes.'

The manager breezed from his car and moved towards the main doors of the cinema. Malcolm leaned out of the window. Click, click, click, went the camera.

'That it?' he asked.

'Sure is.'

I had collected my rogues' gallery, everyone I had spoken to over the first two days was now on film. At least, those I was interested in.

I asked Malcolm when I could expect the photographs.

'A couple of hours. I'll get them processed and send them around. I hope there is something in this for me, mate. The firm's expense and all that.'

I grinned, and punched him on the arm.

*　　　*　　　*

I was back in the library, on the same chair, at the same table, studying the same books brought by the same girl. Only this time it was a little different. Now, I was trying to convince myself that Mrs Richardson's strange experience might be fact, not the other way round. But I was still a confused man when I pushed the books aside and stepped into the sunlight.

*　　　*　　　*

I was in my office. The photographs had arrived. I shuffled them around on the desk, settled them in lines, then changed the lines.

I decided to work on the premise that Karen was dead, that she had indeed been murdered as her mother believed.

So who had reason to murder Karen?

I tapped two photographs in turn.

George Benson? I wasn't buying the story that he shunned Karen because of the gossip their attachment created. He was hardly a public official, a councillor, and there was no wife in the background. So why had he turned his back on the girl? An imponderable at the moment.

Jimmy Keegan? Now Jimmy had one hell of a reason. He knew the girl had spotted him in Harper Street, had ridden there in the back of the van. He is terrified that Jack might find out. And he had stressed the point of not knowing there was a connection between Karen and Eddie Morgan. But what if he had known? What if he returned to the party with Jack and slipped out again. He sees Karen near Morgan's flat. He follows. He gets her into his van—and—. I shivered. And he had been very ready to believe me when I said Karen was dead, and protest his innocence. Did he already know? Did Keegan have the guts to kill? Maybe. Maybe he did have the guts to kill a hysterical girl.

I took the much worn sketch from my pocket and straightened it on the desk.

Eddie Morgan? Did he have reason to murder? He needed the girl. She was terrified and intent on running. In a rage I had no doubt that Morgan possessed the capacity to murder. But where did that murder take place? In the flat? That would mean Irene Downes had lied. But she had lied before. And she wouldn't wish to be implicated in a murder. Had she taken a more active part than

168

she claimed when Karen came to the flat that morning? Another imponderable.

*   *   *

We were back in the café at the top of the arcade. Rage and resentment bubbled behind George Benson's eyes.

'I'll make the call for you, George,' I said quietly. 'The police might be interested in what I have to tell them. And I'm not harassing you. The truth is all I want. The truth about your relationship with Karen. No more crap! You booked in as father and daughter. I find that very strange.'

He avoided my eyes. He stirred the tea in the cup before him. It was already cold. The skin broke on the surface and began to float in lumps.

'She went wild,' he mumbled, and I asked him to speak up. He didn't seem to hear. 'The last time I took her to the Lakes. We booked in as father and daughter because it seemed simpler. No waitresses and maids eyeing us as if we were doing something dirty. We had gone for a stroll and were resting on a crag. She began to sketch. I watched her. I liked to do that. And it was a mere show of affection when I touched her hair. I'd never seen anyone react that way before. She clawed and kicked at me. She used words I thought she was incapable of. There was madness in her eyes. It took a long

169

time to calm her down. She terrified me.'

'And so you decided to break off with her?'

'Not really.' A dry and weary smile touched his lips. 'It was something I'd been thinking about for some time. It seemed she always wanted to be with me, always wanted my attention. I told her we had better see less of each other, but we could still be friends. She didn't seem to understand, and I found it hard to explain to her. I was not her father, that is what it came down to in the end. The experience on the crag was the last straw. But she still clung to me. She kept asking when we would return to the Lakes. That was out. No more weekends.' He paused. 'And I didn't stop speaking to Karen, just the opposite. She stopped speaking to me. She spread the rumours about our weekends. She wanted to hurt me.

'Sally set you wrong, as I thought she might. She repeated to you what I'd told her.'

I sighed. Now was the time to stick the knife in. 'But she came to you in the early hours of that Friday morning, didn't she? She needed help. She believed her life was in danger. So she came to you.'

'No!' The rage was back in his voice. 'She did not! I last saw Karen on that Thursday morning. She hovered near my stall. I looked at her. I thought she was going to speak. She didn't. She turned and walked away.'

'Oh, I think you saw her again, George,' I

170

said harshly. 'The day after. The early hours of Friday morning. She knocks on your door and you let her in. She's sobbing and confused. She's pleading. You are more scared than her, George. You don't want this sick girl in your life. You want to be rid of her. Anything now! Anything to get her out of your life! You don't mean to hurt her. Perhaps you push her and she bangs her head. But she is dead. What did you do with her body, George?'

His fist grazed my chin. The table turned over. There was the clatter of broken china. We were locked in an embrace. His fists pumped at my sides without effect. I held him firm. It took strong arms to drag him off me, hold him in a chair. I caught my breath and forced myself to relax. I was aware of the rage in his eyes, the hate. I gave my name to the owner and told her to send me a bill for my share of the damages, then walked out.

Perhaps George Benson was a murderer, perhaps he wasn't. If he was, it was up to me to prove it.

CHAPTER SEVENTEEN

'You have to be insane! Really, you have to be out of your tiny little mind!'

Irene Downes held the two halves of her dressing gown together with a clenched fist.

Through the gap in the bedroom door I could see the rumpled bed, the form under the sheets, a naked foot peeping out. It hadn't taken her long to get over the passing of Eddie Morgan. She noticed the direction of my gaze and quickly moved to close the door. Her eyes said it was none of my business.

'That's possible, Irene,' I said, sighing. 'But I still think you're a liar.'

'Prove it!' she challenged. 'You just bloody well try and prove it!'

And that I couldn't do, only ponder, and guess.

'I don't think Karen ever left this flat, Irene, not alive anyway.' I wondered what the man in the next room was making of this. 'She came here, hysterical, almost out of her mind, and Eddie silenced her. How did he do it, Irene? A pillow pressed to her face? His bare hands wrapped around her neck?'

'More preposterous all the time.' She flopped down on a chair. The dressing gown opened and she snatched it shut. 'She came here—she left—on her own two feet.'

'Okay,' I said. 'Say I believe you. What is to say she didn't return?'

'She didn't.'

'The body, Irene!' I pressed. 'What did you and Eddie do with the body!'

She almost came for me, fingers clawing. 'What are you accusing me of?'

'You were there, Irene. Karen was dead,

and so Eddie had a body to dispose of. You must have helped him. That is the reason you lied when you said she left. You are involved, Irene.'

'I am involved in nothing. You are insane!'

I changed tack. 'Did she have a holdall with her?'

'How the hell would I know! I didn't see her. I was in the bedroom while she spoke to Eddie. You are still insane!'

Perhaps I was, just a little. But Eddie had a reason to murder, no matter how tenuous. And Irene loved Eddie.

'I'll be back, Irene.'

Her mouth was a thin straight line as I left.

*   *   *

'How could I, you stupid bastard! Do you think I pushed myself there in a wheelchair!'

We were in the hospital wing of the prison. There were bolts on the doors and bars on the windows.

'Time factor, Jimmy,' I said lightly. 'This is how I figured it. You spot Karen in Harper Street and chase her. She slips you. After your trip to Manchester you return to the party. You make sure you are seen, then out you go again. You know Karen is a friend of Morgan's so you head in that direction. You see Karen on the street. You chase her. This time you catch her. You are probably drunk, and she

173

struggles, and you hit her, and hit her.' I leaned back. 'What did you do with her body, Jimmy?'

'Man, you can talk to my solicitor! You lied to me before! The girl isn't dead! Even the bloody fuzz know that. And Jack never caught up with her. You're the only one who thinks she's dead! You're a bloody nutter!'

'Jimmy.' I leaned forward. 'I ought to screw your neck for what you did to that girl.'

'You touch me you bloody madman, and I'll scream my head off.'

I knew he meant it. He had the security of the prison guards built around him. I was on my feet, wondering what I'd get for just one swing of my clenched fist. I decided it wasn't worth it.

'Don't come back.' Keegan's voice followed me. 'I'll have you, Conroy. You bloody well understand that!'

He was nothing, a little comedian who thought stuffing heroin into the arms of kids was a joke. But maybe he had had the guts to end the life of a young woman on a dark street.

*　　　*　　　*

'What the hell are you playing at! Has that little brain of yours finally cracked!'

At the moment, it seemed everybody I came across was obsessed with my sanity, or lack of

174

it. And I didn't like the way Kevin's finger wagged under my nose. I wanted to grab it, and snap it. He was furious, putting it mildly, paying one of his rare visits to my office. His voice went on and on.

'I fixed it for you to see Keegan. And what happens? You threaten to wring his neck.'

'I never touched him.'

'Maybe not. But he's been bending his solicitor's ear. You dropped me in it, old mate.'

'Okay.' I held up my hands. 'I apologise.'

'And there was a fracas in the Waterloo arcade, and your name was mentioned. Are you going around accusing everybody in this town of murdering that girl?'

'Not quite,' I said quietly, meeting his eyes. 'I went to see Karen's parents. Mrs Richardson came close to convincing me again.'

'Oh, hell!' Kevin took a deep breath. 'Don't give me that vision bullshit again.'

'So where is she?' I asked. He didn't respond. 'You were the smart bastard who said she'd show up as soon as she knew Jack Evans had been taken.'

'I was wrong,' he conceded. 'Perhaps you were right on one point. Perhaps she is still scared of the police and law courts. The kid had a rough time. The rape. The trial. And she's also a drug addict. Another reason. Some of them see us as persecutors. Those are good reasons for not coming forward. But I'll tell

175

you this, Frankie boy—there is a boyfriend!'

No boyfriend. But I didn't see much point in repeating myself. He didn't stay.

*   *   *

'It was cruel what you did to my father! I can never forgive you for that!'

'Was it cruel?'

I had no difficulty meeting Sally Benson's accusing eyes. She was taller than me in her heels, and still bra-less.

'He is upstairs now, resting. Do you want to go up and torment him some more?'

I shrugged. 'Not really.'

'I liked you when you first came,' she said. 'I told you the truth as I knew it, and you twisted everything.'

'No, that's not true,' I said. 'He used you. He knew the questions I would ask, and he knew you would repeat what he had told you.'

'You have a fixation!' Her hands waved in the air. 'You are the only one who thinks that Karen is dead!'

I'd been accused of that before. I asked what time she'd returned home on the Thursday she spotted Karen in that van. She studied me a long time before answering.

'I didn't,' she said quietly. 'I stayed with a friend.'

I was beginning to think she was the only honest person I had met lately. I admired that.

'So you don't know if Karen came here that night, or rather, in the early hours of Friday morning?'

'No. I don't. But I know my father would not harm Karen. And he explained why he lied. She frightened him. What if she had one of those fits of rage when there were people about? What would they think my father had done to her? He is nearly forty years older than Karen.'

She showed me to the door, and it slammed behind me. So there was no evidence that Karen came to see George Benson that Friday morning, and no evidence that she didn't. I sighed and walked away.

*   *   *

Monday again; just another day.

Still no Karen. Mrs Harker was back, needles clicking in the outer office. I was doing nothing more than gazing out of the window when it struck me.

I had relieved the itch! I knew the answer to the problem that had troubled me. I knew that Karen was dead! And I knew why she died!

Just a few words spoken in the middle of a long conversation, meaning little at the time, but it had unlocked the mystery.

I was soon out of the office and into my car.

*   *   *

The average age of the class was around twelve. They were very noisy, very messy, and very happy. I envied them. The teacher was one of the modern school, let the kids do their own thing and they will respect you. Myself, I wasn't too sure. He was the same teacher who took Karen's night class. He seemed even bigger than the last time we met. He pumped my hand like we were old mates, then he settled behind his desk.

I placed the photographs before him. 'Could one of these men be the one you saw drop Karen from his car on the night you mentioned?'

'Hard to say.' He puzzled, frowned. 'Like I said, I only remember the eyes, the way they devoured Karen as she walked away.'

He went through the photographs a couple of times. Then he held one to the light. He began to sketch on a sheet of paper. The likeness was reduced to black and white. Then he began to shade. The top and lower half of the face was reduced to shadow, until only the eyes remained. He leaned back, smiled, passed the photograph back.

'That's the one, mate,' he said.

My fingers trembled, my heartbeat quickened, new thoughts and ideas began to churn around my mind. I asked if he was positive.

'I wouldn't like to stand up in court and

swear to it—but I'm sure.'

I thanked him, and was on my way.

*   *   *

Jenny, who lived in the flat next to Karen, sat opposite me in the café across the street from the office where she worked. It took a lot of persuasion to get her to open up. She felt she might be betraying her friends. I wore her down.

'I am not absolutely certain.' She bit her lip. 'But I'd say Ian loved Karen. The way he looked at her, hovered when she was near.'

'And Karen's reaction?' I asked, leaning closer.

'She avoided him.'

'Val's reaction?'

'Muted rage, sorrow.' Jenny continued to chew her lip. 'She never said anything in my presence. She watched them, especially Karen. Val suffered in silence.'

'Did Val and Ian argue?'

'Not that I am aware of.'

'Did Karen and Val argue?'

'They seemed to have ceased speaking, though whether it was anything to do with Ian I'm not sure. And it seemed to be mostly on Karen's part. Val would attempt to start a conversation, but Karen never responded. Val didn't dislike Karen, you have to understand that. I think she loved her. She was

179

undoubtedly hurt by Ian.'

'Was he open in his admiration for Karen?'

'Not exactly,' Jenny said. 'Openly attentive might be more apt. As though he was desperate for her to acknowledge his presence.'

I asked when Ian's obsession had begun.

'Oh, less than a year. He didn't appear interested in her when she first arrived. Ian tends to be rather insular despite his outgoing charm.'

There was more. Her mind was turning, reaching for something. I didn't press.

'A month or so back I walked out of my flat. They were on the landing. Ian glared at me and skulked off. Karen was upset. I asked what was wrong. She said Ian wanted to divorce Val, and marry her. That was it. She went into her flat. It was one of our longer conversations.'

More interesting all the time. I asked her about Ian and Val.

'She is older than him—obviously, and is the real breadwinner. He makes a living at what he does, but nothing more, although he believes he is a genius. Val is also the strong one. I have an idea he would be little more than a lost schoolboy without her.'

I recalled the day we met. She had said something—the itch I had relieved. I put it to her again. Her answer was the same, only this time she went into a more detailed explanation.

There was little more she had to say. She had to get back to the office. I stayed with my thoughts for a while.

*   *   *

I followed him for half an hour, then stopped him on the street. He showed no surprise.

'I'd like a chat, Ian,' I said.

He needed no time to consider. He shrugged mildly. We settled in my car. He patiently waited for me to start the conversation. I took his mind back to the day I asked if he had ever taken Karen to her night class in his car. He remembered.

'You said you never took her, that you didn't even know she attended night school.' I paused. 'Why lie, Ian?'

'Did I lie?' he asked lightly. His face showed nothing. 'You said the man in the car couldn't be identified.'

'I had you photographed, Ian. And now the witness positively identifies you.'

'You have been busy.' He smiled, showed no resentment, stared into the distance. 'Just the one time. I was pulling up outside the house as she came down the steps. It was raining hard, or she would probably have declined.'

'Why lie about something so trivial?'

'The way you put it to me.' The smile never dimmed. 'Ravenous eyes that stripped Karen naked? I decided to stay out of it.'

181

'Did you love her?' I asked quietly.

'I wonder,' he said absently, then his eyes flicked to me for a moment. 'I suppose Jenny has been talking?' No response from me. 'I guess that was inevitable. Jenny never liked me. But yes, in a way I did love Karen. I found her lovely. Soft and curvy, vulnerable, and young. The very opposite to Val. Yes, in a way I did love her.'

'And you offered to leave Val for her?'

'Jenny really does have big ears.' The smile died, the eyes hardened. 'That was a long time ago, or so it seems. I was a fool. Anyway, Karen made it plain she felt nothing for me. My feelings for her died. I love Val. My emotional attachment to Karen was nothing more than a whim.'

Maybe it was, maybe it wasn't. 'How did Val react to your obsession with Karen?'

'That is none of your business!' he snapped.

I was making it my business, but I didn't press on that point. 'What time did Karen return to the house that Friday morning?'

He didn't bother to answer. He was out of the car and striding away.

CHAPTER EIGHTEEN

'Reason to murder, Val,' I was saying. 'You were the only one with sufficient motive.'

Her eyes were cool, her features stony. No emotion showed but for the rigid stiffness of her body as she sat behind the desk, toying with a pencil between her fingers.

'Absurd,' she said coldly. 'Give me that motive.'

'Ian loved Karen.'

'Oh?'

'I suppose Ian recounted the chat we had earlier?' Her unmoving body said yes. 'Karen returned here in the early hours of Friday morning. You already said that was possible. But you insisted you didn't hear or speak to her. Not true, Val. You spoke to her.'

And that was the itch that had plagued me, that simple sentence. It came from Jenny that first Monday when she had stated, 'If Val says Karen didn't return—then Karen didn't return.' Val was an insomniac. Val sat in her living room throughout the long nights. She couldn't fail to hear the front door opening.

'I'll tell you how it was,' I said. 'Karen had lived through a terrifying experience that night. She saw and heard something that she believed placed her life in danger. She had already decided she needed to leave town, and she came home to pack. She had no money. No friends. So who could she turn to? There is only you and Ian. But Karen isn't happy with you. She thinks you have turned against her. You have neglected her, you intend to drag her off to a doctor. She no longer trusts you.

183

'So she knocks and you open the door. She demands to see Ian. She knows he will help. Ian has promised many times to take her away. Ian is willing to leave you. She knows this. She demands to see Ian. Her voice is raised. She tries to push inside the flat but you are stronger. You are in the hall and you begin to struggle. Then you strike her. You pick something off the hall stand and you strike her.' I leaned forward. 'Where is the body, Val?'

She disconcerted me by relaxing. A smile stretched her lips. She shook her head sadly. 'It appears that Mrs Richardson has a companion on her flight of fancy.'

I was losing, and my words quickened. 'There is more, Val. Something I should have spotted earlier. But I was fooled by your obvious affection for Karen, which never wavered, even when Ian began to drool over her. It never did add up. The way you changed stories. The nightmare phone call from Mrs Richardson. The two men who called here and said Karen had something that belonged to them. The fact that Karen was a drug addict. You loved her, Val. You should have been frantic with worry. You should have been on the phone yourself, screaming to the police. But you were not worried. You were cool and calm. You said Karen would appear, though you knew different. In fact, you knew the girl was dead.

'And there was this rubbish about Karen saying she was leaving on the Thursday evening. That was a lie. You were keeping your options open. You said you hadn't actually seen her leave, that she might have come back later for her holdall. That was insurance in case Jenny or one of the other tenants heard her return. Much better for you if nobody knew Karen returned that morning.' She remained mute. 'You are an insomniac, Val. You were in the living room when Karen returned in the early hours of Friday. You must have heard her.' I deviated from the truth. 'The light was burning. I can prove it.'

She sighed, pulled in a deep breath.

'All right,' she said quietly. 'She returned. I did speak to her.'

At last! 'And?'

'She was incoherent. I thought she was hallucinating. I shook her, but it didn't help. She claimed that men were chasing her, that they meant to kill her. She asked me to drive her out of town. I refused. She was a sick girl.'

That she was. 'And?'

'She ran upstairs and came down with the holdall. She said she was leaving.'

I smiled drily. 'And you let her go?'

'I did. But I thought she'd be back. I thought she was playing one of her silly games to make me feel sorry for her. I thought she would be back inside an hour. She wasn't. I was angry with her. I even pushed a few pound

185

notes into her hand.'

'If she left,' I stressed. 'Why the lie?'

'For the same reasons I mentioned the last time we spoke. The lie was for the benefit of the Richardsons, to prevent them learning of Karen's addiction, a lie I compounded with you. What would they have thought if I'd told them how Karen came to leave? In the middle of the night, raving and distraught. It would have increased their anxiety a hundredfold. The nightmare would have paled to insignificance.'

'And now you know why Karen was afraid— you know about the arrest of Jack Evans?'

'Of course,' she replied. 'But how was I to know that Karen had good reason to be afraid? Her story didn't make sense. And the police have been here, and yes, I lied to them. I told them I had not seen Karen leave, that I last saw her on the Thursday evening.'

'Why?' I asked wearily.

'Because once you begin to lie, it is hard to escape from that lie. How could I explain why I had lied earlier? It would have sounded as if I had something to hide.'

'Something to hide—like murder?'

'You are welcome to pull up the floorboards,' she offered drily.

It was an offer I might accept, later. 'You knew that Ian loved her?'

Just a snap of anger crept into her voice. 'He didn't love her. He loved the idea of loving her. Men felt a need to protect her, as did Ian. It was something I understood.'

'He's a lot younger than you, Val.' I tried to get under her skin. 'Twelve years? You love him. And by hell you mean to keep him. Even if it turned you into a murderess.'

She stood, came around the desk and opened the door.

'Good day, Mr Conroy. You have heard the truth. Karen returned here sometime around three. She left some twenty minutes later. I have no idea where she went. I do know she is still very much alive.'

The door slammed behind me.

*   *   *

Almost three-thirty in the morning, and I stood on the pavement outside the Spencer house. A light burned in the living room window behind me. The night was pitch black, filled with the howling wind and rain that had returned in the late evening.

If Val had told the truth, it had to have been this way for Karen that morning. The timing was right.

Where would Karen make for?

She is alone, friendless, and cold. Fear has driven back the cravings of her body for heroin. But still, her mind is sluggish. The streets frighten her. She believes she is being hunted. She keeps clear of the main roads. I would have headed for the motorway interchange where the lorries thundered throughout the night and used my thumb, but that wasn't Karen's style.

I began to walk, down twisting alleys and across narrow streets. I encountered no night people. I was accompanied only by the hollow ring of my own footsteps, my vaporised breath, the drumming of the rain.

The bus station stood empty, dark, the only glimmer of light coming from the illuminated charts and maps on the wall. I checked the time table. Nothing. The first bus arrived at six.

I walked again, not far to go.

I moved at a moderate pace, the pace I guessed to be that of a frightened girl carrying a bag; short steps, air rasping in her lungs, eyes constantly flickering over her shoulder for danger.

I found the railway station in partial darkness. It had never been much of a station, and in the sixties the axe had fallen. But the goods trains still chugged through, and the odd passenger train. It was always manned.

I gripped the tall steel gate and shook it, yelled high and loud. Several minutes elapsed before the dark figure emerged. He was round and tubby, his peaked cap twisted at an eccentric angle. He came closer, squinted to examine my face in the dim light. His voice was gruff.

'No trains tonight, mate!'

'Stuff the bloody trains,' I replied.

I clamped my eyes shut as a sudden light blinded me, then he dipped his torch. He said something about me being Frank Conroy the rugby player and that he had known my mum. But that was no great deal. She had lots of friends. Long past were the days when I looked into the eyes of strangers and wondered if they might be my father. I pushed the photograph of Karen through the bars and he examined it in the light of his torch.

'Around this time,' I told him. 'Friday the fourth.'

'That's about right,' he mumbled.

He handed the photograph back, and I knew Val hadn't lied. Karen had left the house when Val said. I wasn't sure if the information pleased me or not. I only knew I wanted to see an end to this business, one way or the other.

'Rattled the gates like you,' the man went on. 'Wanted to know the time of the next train. I asked where she wanted to go. She said anywhere. I told her eight o'clock. She seemed disappointed.' He scratched his head under the cap. 'Odd girl, arriving at that time, humping a bag, no particular destination in mind. Said she only had eight pounds. Didn't look well either, so I asked her if she'd like to come inside for a cup of tea. She mumbled something about not wanting to hang around. You'd have thought the devil was on her shoulder.'

Very poetic, and very close to the truth. The devil was on Karen's shoulder that morning.

I asked, 'What did she do then?'

'She hesitated, then moved to the phone box.' He pointed. 'She made a call. It didn't take long. She had me a bit worried so I shouted to ask if she was okay. She nodded, said a friend was coming to pick her up at the bridge. I watched her wander off.'

'The railway bridge?' I asked.

'That's what I thought at first.' He pointed to a gap in the buildings across the road. 'But that's the way she headed. Must have meant the bridge on the common.'

'That's an odd place to be picked up,' I said absently. 'You can't get a car up there.'

'Maybe this friend had a tandem.'

I ignored his wit. 'She didn't use a directory, a notebook when she made that phone call?'

'No.'

I thanked him. I followed the route Karen had taken. I was soon treading the damp grass of the common. Small mounds, cut by pathways of mud, a few bushes and trees. I reached the wooden footbridge and paused, stared down into the black void.

There had once been a pond down there, a stagnant smelly pit where the brave kids played. But one of those kids had drowned in six feet of slime. The pond was drained. The hole it left became a dumping ground for

190

anything that could be carried in a cardboard box or pushed in a wheelbarrow. The area around the bridge now stank like hell.

I checked my watch. Three minutes past four. I shivered. I needed no psychic message to tell me Karen had stood on this very spot.

I lit a cigarette, then tossed it away, watched it arc in the darkness and die. My knee began to ache and I gritted my teeth.

I heard him approach and smiled. I twisted round. I knew there had to be someone!

He came to a hesitant stop five yards away. He yanked back on the leash he gripped in his right fist. The Alsation snarled and showed its fangs. The man studied me warily.

'Okay, brother. Keep a tight hold on that monster.' I pulled out my wallet and flicked it open. There was no way he could make out what it contained in this light. Bluntly, I snapped, 'Police.'

I felt him relax, something he seemed to transmit to the dog. It ceased to growl.

I gave him some of the old spiel about looking for a young woman, who just might have been on the common at a certain time on a certain day. I described Karen. He nodded.

'Standing where you are now. Only she looked the other way—across the common to the road.'

I asked if he had spoken to her. A mistake. Too blunt. He was wary again, a tremor in his voice.

191

'Why? What happened to her? I didn't—'

I calmed him down with the right words. He began to talk.

'She looked terrified when she first saw me, then relaxed. I asked if she was all right. She nodded. She said she was waiting for a friend, that she'd be here soon.'

'She?' I couldn't hide the excitement from my voice. 'The friend she waited for was a woman?'

'That's what I gathered.' The man nodded. 'It seemed very odd but it wasn't my place to interfere. I walked away. I came back about fifteen minutes later and she was gone.'

I asked if he had seen anyone else that morning.

'No.' A definite reply, then a hesitation. 'I did hear something as I came back over the bridge. A noise below. The dog growled.' He paused. 'I heard a scream some minutes before. A cat, or some other animal, I thought.'

He thought wrong. I collected his name and address and he went on his way. I studied my watch. The time read four-fourteen.

Oh, Jesus! Maybe she was down there someplace, buried in that filth. I was utterly weary. I wiped away the tear that ran down my cheek. It wasn't bloody fair! It shouldn't have happened. Half a dozen people could have helped her that day. More if you counted the police. So why hadn't she gone to them when she ran from Jack Evans and his band, when she believed they meant to damage or even kill her? Was she scared of the police? Definitely! Probably more scared of them than Jack Evans.

I walked from the common with a weary heart.

In the darkness of my office I sat alone and pondered. I had at last established Karen's movements from the time she arrived at the Evans house with Keegan.

12.15 am: Evans and Keegan seen leaving the party and getting into the van.

12.30 am: Harper Street. Karen leaves the van and is spotted. She runs.

2.00 am: Morgan's flat. She recounts what she has seen, appeals for help. He is intent on his own profit.

3.00 am: Home. Talks to Val. Leaves.

3.45 am: The railway station.

4.00 am: The bridge on the common.

4.14 am: Poor Karen.

The times were not exact, but close enough.

One last problem. If Karen was buried under the rubble on the common—who took her life? Who had she telephoned from the station and arranged to meet?

I could only come up with one name—Val Spencer.

The person Karen expected to meet on that bridge was a woman. It could only have been Val.

I tried to work out what had happened.

Karen had left the house, intent on leaving town. She was disorientated. She probably didn't even know what day it was. No buses, no trains. She is afraid that Jack Evans will find her. She needs transport—a friend. She is at the railway station. She is too weary to walk back to the house, and Jack Evans might already be there. She uses the telephone. Val answers and Karen demands to speak to Ian. No deal. Val means to preserve her marriage. She knows that if Karen reaches Ian it will be over. So she decides to meet Karen. She suggests Karen waits at the bridge. She kills Karen in a fit of jealous rage. Love had turned to hate.

It had to have gone something like that.

I picked up the phone and dialled Kevin at home.

CHAPTER NINETEEN

The walls were grey, the door stout, the furniture, which consisted of a plain wooden table and two chairs, was heavy and scarred. The ashtray in front of me overspilled, an empty cigarette packet crumpled beside it. The man opposite showed not a flicker of emotion. The light from the naked bulb overhead reflected from his balding head. He was a Detective Chief Inspector. No one had given me his name.

'So when did you reach the conclusion that Karen Richardson had been murdered?' he asked for something like the fourth time.

My reply was the same. 'I didn't. Just a gut feeling that something was wrong.'

'This gut feeling—there had to be something more substantial behind it than the vision of an elderly woman.'

I no longer knew what I thought. I shrugged. I glanced at my watch, tried to figure out if it was morning or evening. I wondered why I was getting the heavy treatment. Routine, I guessed. Never take anything for what it appears on the surface. We talked on. The minutes dragged slowly. Finally, something that bore an uncanny likeness to a smile touched his mouth. He shuffled the papers in front of him then rose to his feet.

'Follow me.'

I did. Across the corridor to a room much the same as the one we had just left, but for an electric fan heater that droned in a corner. A stenographer sat by the door. A man in shirtsleeves sat at the table. Opposite sat Val Spencer. She seemed to have aged twenty years since the last time I saw her; deep lines etched around her mouth, eyes sunken. I felt a twinge of pity as her voice fought to hold back the choking tears. She didn't seem aware of the new presence in the room.

195

'Karen arrived at the house and knocked on my door. She was dishevelled and distraught. I concluded she was drugged. She repeated over and over that men were chasing her. I didn't believe her. She asked me to drive her out of town. I refused. She went to her flat to pack, then returned. Again she asked me to drive her away. I was angry at her stupidity. When she asked for money I pushed a few pound notes into her palm. I told her to leave if that was the way she felt. She did. But I expected her back inside an hour.

'Some time later the phone rang. Karen. I wasn't surprised. There were no buses or trains. I asked what she expected at that time of the morning. She begged me to come for her in the car and drive her away. I told her to walk back to the house and we would talk it over rationally. She said she couldn't. She asked if anyone had come to the house looking for her. I decided she was paranoid. She said she'd wait at the bridge on the common of all places. Before I could refuse she hung up. I had no intention of going for her. She walked there, she could walk back.

'That's when Ian came from the bedroom. The telephone had woken him. He asked who it was. I told him everything. How Karen had come back, what she said.'

Val rested. Her face fell into her hands for a while. Eyes locked on the table, she began to talk again.

'Ian decided to go for her. We argued. Suddenly, I knew he was going to leave me. I had thought his infatuation with Karen was over. It wasn't. He wanted her, not me. He left in the car.

'He was soon back. There was blood on his hands. He put his head to my breast and cried. He said he had killed Karen. He had hit her and she had fallen and banged her head. He had hidden her body and come back to me.' Val nearly choked. 'I knew fear then, real terror. Ian wanted to go to the police. I persuaded him to wait. Nothing could bring Karen back. He hadn't meant to kill her. I needed time to think.

'Then there was the phone call from Mrs Richardson.' Val's eyes came up. 'How could she know! How could she possibly know that Karen was dead! I could come up with no rational explanation. I pretended to check her flat, then said Karen had mentioned leaving the night before. I couldn't give the true circumstances of Karen's departure. And that was the lie I was stuck with. Then the two men called at the house. At first I thought they were policemen. It was all I could do to prevent myself asking when they had found Karen's body. Of course they were not policemen, as soon became apparent.

'I began to think. What if Karen had not been hallucinating? What if the men she spoke of were actually chasing her? It was something to ponder on. Everything seemed to be dying down when that man Conroy appeared.'

I could hardly believe my ears. She was accusing Ian of Karen's murder. The Chief Inspector touched my elbow, and signalled me to follow.

Another room much the same as the others. A different cast. Ian Spencer appeared cool and calm, as if he'd shaved and showered after emerging from a good night's sleep. His voice was deep, without emotion.

'I went to meet Karen. I was elated. She wouldn't shun me now. She needed me. I loved her so my insides screamed. But it went wrong as soon as I approached her on that bridge. I saw terror and hatred in her eyes. I tried to reassure her. I told her I would look after her. She kept asking why Val hadn't come. I tried to put my arm around her.' He wiped a hand across his cheek. 'She spat at me. She began to kick and claw. Then she screamed. I was scared. I wanted to stop that scream. I hit her and she fell. Everything went quiet. I stooped. I touched her face. My hand came away bloody. I knew she was dead. I think I carried her body down the banking. It's all a bit blurred. It was an accident. I loved her.'

I'd heard enough. I made my way to Kevin's office. I'd been there an hour, smoking, talking in circles.

'Why was I given the heavy treatment?' I

asked.

He shrugged. 'The Chief has little faith in visions.'

'I got it wrong,' I said sourly. 'I'd have bet my life on Val Spencer. She had the clearest motive—the preservation of her marriage.'

'You've been wrong before, mate.' He smiled.

'What will Ian get?' I asked.

Another shrug. 'He'll probably go for a plea of manslaughter. He'll serve a few years, whichever way it goes.'

'And Val will be waiting,' I said wearily. 'And maybe I should have fingered him earlier. The air of indifference he affected when he spoke of Karen. He was always so cool and collected, always that boyish smile. Until it became clear that Val had lied, I never gave a thought to either of the Spencers. As I said, he seemed indifferent to Karen. And Val was obviously fond of the girl, caring. But there were several pointers to them.'

'Which only became apparent when you took the view that Karen was dead,' Kevin said. He stressed, 'And nobody knew that.'

'No. But once Jack Evans was in custody and she didn't surface, I decided to try again, work along the theory that she was dead. I had everybody connected with Karen photographed. I stared at those bloody photographs for hours hoping for a sudden flash of enlightenment. None came. I narrowed the suspects down to three for a while.

'Jimmy Keegan was never really on. Okay, he could have known that Karen knew Morgan. He could have been waiting outside Morgan's flat that morning, picked her up as she left. But that would mean Karen had spoken to Morgan, that Keegan would have to do something about Morgan. He didn't. Morgan's phone call to Jack Evans came out of the blue as far as he was concerned.

'Then there was George Benson. God knows what their relationship was. Maybe as innocent as he claimed. But whatever, it turned sour. And Karen in desperation just might have knocked on his door that morning, and he just might—

'Then there was Eddie Morgan. Short tempered and vicious. He just might have hit the girl too hard, and Irene Downes just might have been prepared to cover up for him. But then, next morning Morgan was a happy man, thinking of what Karen had told him. Not the attitude of a man who had committed murder only hours before.

'And the holdall. Karen wasn't carrying the holdall that Thursday night. So unless she stashed it someplace, which was unlikely, she had to have returned to the Spencer house for it. It depended when. After she left Harper Street? That was what I thought at first. Harper Street, her flat, to Eddie Morgan's.

The holdall was missing so she had to have it with her when she died. But eventually, Val gave me the timings. Karen arrived back around three, after she had seen Eddie Morgan. And Karen wasn't interested in packing. She had few clothes and no treasured possessions. The decision to pack was an afterthought. I got it wrong there. Karen went back to the house to appeal to Val, not Ian. And Karen wanted Val to feel sorry for her, as Val said. The little waif stepping into the storm with her belongings in a single bag. So if Val hadn't lied, and Karen had left the house, I guessed at the route she'd take and followed it.

'No trains. She made a call from the station. Another plea. She said she'd wait for Val at the bridge and hung up before Val had time to answer. She fully expected Val to come for her. But Ian appeared.

'And Karen was an unstable girl. That was the key, even discounting the drugs and all she had been through that night. She had fits, threw tantrums that were hard to control. It was a self-protective mechanism she had developed when she felt in danger. Ian triggered it. She opened her mouth and screamed. Ian said it scared him. I believe him. George Benson had a similar experience with her.'

Kevin had listened without interruption. He stretched.

'Maybe,' he said. 'But we haven't heard the

whole truth yet. Val said she stopped Ian coming to the police. Yet he had taken the trouble to hide the body. And the Spencers have something against them that won't go down too well with a jury, and could put Val inside with him.'

He waited for my eyes to meet his. I knew he was about to drop a bombshell.

'The next night they went back for the body,' he said quietly. My mouth fell open. 'That's right. The body wasn't on the common. It is somewhere on the moors. We have a team out there now. Val Spencer decided to make sure the body was never found. She did the thinking, he went along. He was a weak and gutless bastard. She was both mother and lover.'

'So how did—?'

'I'm coming to that, mate. When you rang at six in the morning with that weird story about Karen being buried under the rubbish tip on the common, I thought you'd finally gone off your rocker. But you are an old mate, so I took along a couple of lads and we did some digging. We found no body, but we did find a bloodstained holdall. Ian had tossed it off the bridge, and the next night he and Val couldn't find it. It was easy after that. They didn't take long to break.'

I nodded, happy that it was over, saddened that a young woman had lost her life. I guessed Karen was just unlucky, especially with the characters she met. We had little more to say to each other. I plodded home.

*   *   *

I lay on the divan. The only light in the room a diffused yellow as it filtered in from the street outside, and the glow of the cigarette between my fingers. I heard a chorus of tuneless carols drifting upwards as the drunks made their way home.

The Richardsons already had the news when I called on them. They didn't seem unduly shaken, only relieved that it was over, for they always knew that their daughter had died. They were saddened that Val Spencer had been involved in that death.

Anyway, Karen was at rest; the deed was done and the tears dried out.